Bedroom Blarney

by

Cynthia Breeding

This is a work of fiction. Names, characters, places, and incidents are either the product of the author's imagination or are used fictitiously, and any resemblance to actual persons living or dead, business establishments, events, or locales, is entirely coincidental.

Bedroom Blarney

COPYRIGHT © 2022 by Cynthia Breeding

Cover Art by *Tina Lynn Stout*

The Wild Rose Press, Inc.
PO Box 708
Adams Basin, NY 14410-0708
Visit us at www.thewildrosepress.com

Publishing History
First Edition, 2023
Trade Paperback ISBN 978-1-5092-4828-5
Digital ISBN 978-1-5092-4829-2

Published in the United States of America

She flipped on her computer when she got to her room and checked the school's email. Faculty and staff were forbidden to use Blog-Face—or any other social media—on school computers, so what was there was mundane, at best. Faculty meeting after school on Tuesday, Parent-Teachers night on Thursday, and a message from one of the counselors to come to her office during planning time. Probably a new student enrolling. Deer Hill's policy was to give teachers as much background information as administration had on new students to help them fit in.

What Eve wasn't prepared for when she got to the counselor's office later was finding Brenda Caldwell waiting. What was Brian's wife doing here?

Chapter One

"Vodka martini, extra dry. Two olives."

"Yes, ma'am. Coming right up."

As the bartender moved away to get her drink, Eve O'Connor closed her wet umbrella, plopped it alongside her satchel on the empty barstool next to her, and pinched the bridge of her nose to relieve tension. TGIF had never sounded so good. If she were the superstitious type, she'd think Loki, the Nordic god of mischief, had been trailing her all day. Her art classes had been crap. Not one high school kid had taken notes on value and hue in color, and they certainly had not cared about line and space in composition. Or Viking gods, whose sculptures had been the object of today's lesson.

Given the array of video games on smart phones and tablets, it was getting harder to get her students interested—let alone keep them interested—in something as mundane as classical art. Little wonder newbie teachers lasted less than two years in many cases. She had even contemplated changing careers herself, but Joe, her worthless ex-husband, had gambled away her savings before she'd caught him, and she was still paying off the cost of the divorce. Besides, she had almost ten years invested in Deer Hill High School.

"Why so glum?" a male voice asked behind her. "It is Friday, after all."

Eve turned to find her friend, Chad Olson, grinning

at her as he pulled out the stool on her other side. Adonis good-looking, with sun-streaked blond hair and nearly cobalt-colored eyes, he was already being checked out by the few women in the bar this early. Combined with his athletic football-coach build, Eve suspected he wouldn't be here long before one of the ladies sent over a drink.

"I'm just tired," she said as the bartender placed the martini in front of her and automatically started her tab. "Rough week."

"I hear you. Reynolds sprained an ankle in practice yesterday, and the game with O.U. is tomorrow."

"Your starting quarterback?" The only reason Eve followed college football was because Chad was a coach for Dallas-Fort Worth Metro University. "What will you do? I thought that game was supposed to be close."

"It is. Sims is going to have to fill in. Makes me glad I'm not the head coach, though. If we lose, he's going to take a lot of heat." Chad's phone beeped, alerting him he had a Blog-Face message. His face turned dark as he read it. "Damn it."

"Problem?"

"Just my wife wanting to know when I'll be home." He slipped the phone back into his pocket without replying and took a big swig of the beer the bartender had brought. "I'm getting sick of being nagged."

Eve nibbled on one of the olives at the end of her toothpick and glanced over. "Angelina probably just wants some adult company."

"If I believed that, maybe I'd go home. All she does is dote on the kid, though."

"Why don't you get a sitter and go out to dinner? Make it a romantic evening."

Chad grimaced. "The last time we tried that, she kept calling home every ten minutes. For Christ's sake, Jessica is almost two."

At least Eve didn't have *that* problem. Joe hadn't been inclined toward fatherhood, and maybe Fate had smiled on her that she hadn't gotten pregnant. And, at thirty-two, she didn't feel an urge for single motherhood either. Children were cute, as long as they were someone else's.

The bartender set another beer down in front of Chad and inclined his head. "From the brunette over there."

"Thanks." Chad turned and smiled at the woman, lifting the stein in salute. She inhaled, lifting half-exposed breasts, and smiled back. He turned back to Eve. "Looks like a score. Maybe I should cancel my other appointment."

"Other appointment?"

Chad tapped the phone in his shirt pocket. "Met a girl on Blog-Face last week."

"How many does that make?"

"A few." He shrugged. "Less than ten anyway. I don't keep them around long enough for anyone to dig her claws into me."

Eve motioned to the bartender for another martini. "Just a thought, but I don't suppose you mention you're married?"

"Why should I? I'm just getting a little action. I don't lead anyone on." He looked at the brunette and winked. She winked back. "You see?" he said to Eve, "it's an open invitation. Why turn it down?"

"Well, Angelina is waiting. Besides, the brunette looks hardly old enough to be legal." She knew that sounded snide, but she couldn't help herself.

Chad frowned. "What's gotten into you? You're seeing Caldwell—my *married* boss—so it's not exactly like you're wearing a halo."

"That's different."

He arched a brow. "Really? How so?"

Eve sipped her martini before answering. "I knew Brian was married. He was upfront about it."

"A fact he could hardly hide, since you met his wife at the same party."

"True, but his kids are older, and Brenda is involved with so many charities, she's hardly ever home. It's not like I'm interfering with their marriage."

His eyebrow rose higher. "Did you discuss it with her?"

Eve felt her cheeks warm. "Of course not. The point is, I am not looking for commitment or another husband, so she has nothing to worry about. I like having sex, though. Is that so wrong? A married lover is very safe. Neither of us has expectations beyond a good time in bed."

"I'll agree with you there," Chad said and set his empty mug down. "And, if you'll excuse me, I think I'll go see about showing that little brunette over there a very good time."

It didn't take long before Chad and the woman left, and Eve turned back to the bartender, signaling for her third—and last—martini. Besides having to drive home, she had to count calories these days as well.

The place was filling up. Lots of twenty-something men, some dressed in white shirts and ties, indicating they worked in downtown financial institutions, and others in more casual khaki and polo shirts, who probably were IT people. Practically every one of them was tapping away at their smart phones, only glancing up to nod at the bartender or sweep the room in search of possible women to score with.

No man's look lingered on her, even though she was sitting at the end of the bar in plain view, wearing a pale blue silk blouse with an extra button undone. Eve knew she was not unattractive. Plenty of men had said her curvy body was enticing, as was her long auburn hair and tilted greenish-blue eyes—although, come to think on it, that had been when *she* was in her twenties.

God, she felt suddenly old. These days, only Brian complimented her. At forty-five, he thought she was young. Besides, he definitely had an ulterior motive for making her feel sexy. Not that she objected.

Eve pulled out her own cell phone and tapped her Blog-Face account. Skipping the public Bulletin Board, she turned on the private settings and clicked on Personal Notes. The last conversation with Brian—a rather lurid comment on their next meeting—popped up. She smiled. Who said pornographic allusions only turned men on? She found his suggestions titillating. Rereading his last message, she felt herself getting hot. Hitting the response button, she quickly typed:

—Are we on for tonight?—

She leaned against the curved back of the bar stool. If she thought about it, most of these young guys probably couldn't hold their own against someone like Brian. As athletic director for the university, he still kept himself physically fit. His stamina—a trait Eve cherished in a man—was truly incredible. Their sessions left her completely exhausted and totally satiated, probably because Brian took great pride in making sure she came, over and over. Probably egotism on his part, but she sure as heck wasn't complaining. With his full head of black hair, only beginning to silver at his sideburns, Brian didn't look much older than these young guys, either. He'd sent her a selfie from his pool this summer showing muscular biceps and his hard-ridged six-pack belly. Unfortunately, the lower part of him wasn't clear under the water, but she had a sneaking suspicion he'd been nude. Eve squirmed on her chair, feeling moist heat between her legs. Lord, she wanted sex tonight.

Her phone beeped. She practically panted as she picked it up.

—Not tonight, babe. Gotta take the wife to a reception.—

Eve swallowed her disappointment along with the remainder of her martini. Slowly, she gathered her bag and slid off the stool. She was *so* ready, but it looked to be another night with the pink bunny instead of a man. She sighed as she left the bar. At least the rain had turned into light mist.

A married lover might be safe and highly inclined to please her, but being involved with one was a trade-off.

He wasn't always available when she needed him.

****

Molly Whitefield put the Chinese take-out cartons on the kitchen counter of her tiny apartment and turned on her Bose Wave. Instantly, the soothing sounds of ocean surf filled the room, reminding her of the Hawaiian cruise she'd taken with her mother last summer. Molly'd fallen in love with the islands. She inhaled deeply, letting the stress flow from her body.

It had been a hectic Friday. Being the front desk

clerk at Deer Hill High School was always busy, but today had been pure chaos. The left side of the bleachers had reeked of marijuana during the morning pep rally, causing administrators to herd a flock of twenty-five to thirty students into the office. The school's P.D. had been summoned and parents called—most of whom were insistent that *their* sons and daughters certainly could not be involved in the incident. Shortly after lunch, an attorney for one of the students had shown up, claiming discrimination and demanding to know which of the group had past histories with drugs. After Molly explained the school did not release that kind of information, the attorney had berated her for being rude and gone to Mrs. Wilson, the principal—a short-tempered woman who had little patience for trouble from her faculty or staff. Molly, who had won the title of "Miss Congeniality" at her high school prom, had received a reprimand via email shortly after the man left. And then, in a fitting finish to a fine day, someone set off a stink bomb in the centrally located library, the fumes of which wafted quickly throughout the duct system, causing students to text home and bring another angry horde of parents to the front desk.

Picking up one of the cartons and the free, cheap chopsticks, Molly went into the living room, kicked her shoes off, and sank onto the sofa. She switched to a favorite CD and smiled. When she was growing up, her gran never tired of telling her about the Second British Invasion of the Sixties. She had made it all sound so real, Molly wished she could have experienced it herself. Between herself and Gran, they owned every album—original and digitally released—of the leaders of the Invasion.

Molly picked a small piece of pork out of the container. She probably should not have ordered something that was mainly rice, since she had a perennial fifteen pounds to lose, but it was comfort food. Since she hadn't heard from Chad, the guy she'd met on-line last week, a long Friday night stretched ahead.

Chad. She loved saying his name aloud. It had such a good ring to it. He sounded like a really nice guy, asking about her interests and telling her they mirrored his own. At first, she'd been hesitant even to get on Blog-Face, but one of the other single secretaries had assured her it was safe. Since Molly didn't frequent bars—she knew her sensible clothes, brownish hair, and plain looks wouldn't excite anyone amidst false-eyelashed glam girls in stilettos—she felt she had a better chance connecting in a more private manner.

She hadn't met Chad in person yet, but she hoped she would soon. Actually, she had been hoping he'd leave her a message on Blog-Face about this weekend. The rain was supposed to let up, and she had hinted about meeting at the Fort Worth Zoo. She'd told him about the wonderful zoo in Honolulu, and he'd agreed he liked wild animals too. So far, though, she'd heard nothing. Just for good measure, she picked up her phone and checked her account, but the last message from him had been two days before.

Putting it down, she wondered what other twenty-two-year-old single women did on Friday nights in Dallas—the ones who weren't doing the bar scene, that is. She really didn't know her way around the city too well, having just moved in August from a small town near Kerrville, where her German ancestors had settled in the nineteenth century. Her parents had not wanted her to move, nor had Tommy, her high-school boyfriend who was actually more of a brother than sweetheart, but she'd felt the need to get away, to see what city life had to offer.

To find out what city men were like.

Molly finished her take-out and turned on the TV, placing her phone beside the remote. Maybe Chad would message her later.

She hoped so. He sounded so nice.

****

Brian Caldwell stabbed into his piece of tasteless fowl and sighed. Yet another fund-raising charity dinner with the politically correct choice of rubber chicken—heaven forbid some entity would serve beef or pork—and no alcohol. How many more of these drawn-out dinners with keynote speakers preaching to their own choirs did his wife have obligations to attend? He'd lost track of how many "committees" she served on, but it seemed, with the holiday season not far off, every one of them was bound and determined to increase whatever monetary goals they'd set.

Not that he had anything against charities. He'd written a number of large checks to most of his wife's endeavors—albeit some of the monies came from his department's slush fund. He just didn't want to have to sit at dinners eating catered food that had lingered too long beneath heat lamps to have any taste or texture.

Taste and texture. Brian smothered a grin. His mistress had both. He loved running his hands up Eve's long, satiny legs, which hadn't turned to cellulite yet, and tasting her. Feasting on a naked Eve was far better than sitting at another stuffy dinner, formally clad in suit and tie.

"What's so funny?" Brenda asked.

"Nothing," he said quickly. "I was just thinking about a joke one of the coaches told at the office."

"Football humor, I suppose," she said, turning her attention back to her plate.

More like cheerleader humor, but Brian didn't say it. Hell, Eve made a darn good private cheerleader. Not only was she willing to experiment, she even encouraged him. He'd never known another woman who actually enjoyed watching porn videos—certainly not his Brown University-educated wife.

He glanced over at Brenda. Tall and still slender at forty-nine, she wore her platinum hair pulled neatly back into some kind of configuration, silhouetting the long line of her neck and revealing the classic profile of her face with its straight, aristocratic nose. When he'd met her, the summer in Newport between his junior and senior year at college, he thought she looked as regal as Princess Diana. Now his wife was more Ice Queen than princess.

He wasn't even sure when he actually started thinking of Brenda like that. When they'd first married, he'd been so captivated by having made an Ivy-League catch to brag about to his Aggie friends he had chalked up his wife's reticence in bed as due to being the coddled, protected daughter of a wealthy New York banker. The first son had come along in fairly short order—another braggart moment—with a second one several years later, although that one was constantly in trouble at high school. Brenda had become more involved with raising the boys than she was with him or his career. Gradually, their sex life dwindled down to a rare obligation.

But Eve appreciated his virility and endurance. His

thoughts drifted back to Eve, and he excused himself to go to the restroom. Once there, he logged on to Insta-Blog.

—Sure wish I were eating you tonight, babe.—

True to BF claims, her return message was instantaneous.

—I could be dessert.—

On his way back to the table, Brian briefly contemplated making some excuse after dinner of having left something at the office, then decided against it. Brenda normally didn't question him if he came home late—having drinks with his coaching staff was a long-standing tradition—but he didn't want to arouse her suspicions.

As he sat down, his eyes fixed on the black sheath Brenda wore—or more precisely, on the V-neckline that was lower cut than usual, revealing a hint of cleavage. Why had he not noticed that before? Generally, her dresses were conservative, keeping everything interesting covered. Was she sending him a signal this evening?

Brenda looked up so suddenly, he thought for a moment he had asked the question aloud. She opened her mouth to say something and then realized where his gaze had been. Slowly, she smiled, breaking the façade of Ice Queen as warmth lit her blue eyes, and she handed him her cake, letting her hand brush his as he took the plate.

Hell, maybe he was going to get some *real* dessert after all.

Chapter Two

"Why are you so late?" Angelina asked plaintively when Chad walked in the front door to their house in Garland later that night. "I thought we might have dinner together."

"Sorry," he said, noticing a tomato stain on her T-shirt that looked like a small hand had smeared spaghetti on Angie. "You know how Fridays are—the guys get together before the Saturday game."

"I finally ordered a pizza around seven, but yours is cold now."

Pizza was the other food option they usually had. Unfortunately for a woman who came from an Italian background, there had been no "Mama Mia" in Angie's household who had taught her to cook. "It's okay. I grabbed something on the way home." He looked around. "Where's Jessica?"

"In bed." Her voice had a slight edge. "It's nine-thirty."

Jesus. He hadn't meant to stay out that late. The brunette had been nearly insatiable. He suspected he'd be seeing a lot more of her.

"Sorry," he said again, moving to give Angie a quick kiss on the cheek and noting a sour scent on her shirt as well. "I think I'll go to bed myself since we have the O.U. game tomorrow. I just need to check a couple of things on the computer first."

Before Angie could pick an argument, he strode down the hall to the bedroom that had been converted to an office. "I'll be up soon," he called back before he shut the door.

As he entered his password and logged onto Blog-Face, he thought of Eve's suggestion that he take Angie out for a romantic dinner. How romantic was a wife who smelled like spit-up? And when was the last time she'd worn make-up? And, for that matter, when was the last time they'd had a conversation about anything not related to children? Diaper rash and baby formula weren't his favorite topics.

How could she have changed so much in the five years they'd been married? Hell, they were both thirty, but she was going on fifty.

He shook his head as his profile page popped up. His friends had warned him that once a baby arrived, he'd be relegated to second place. Not that his kid wasn't cute—she'd inherited her mother's dark hair and his blue eyes—but she needed attention one hundred percent of the time, or at least it seemed she did. Sex with Angie had become intermittent quickies, when the baby wasn't screaming or Angie wasn't too tired.

No wonder he'd become a bar-fly.

The thought of which brought him back to his profile page, and he hit Edit. If he intended to see the brunette often—and he did—he needed to create a better profile story. No sense in having her—Tammy... Tara...no, *Tanya*, she'd said her name was—find out who he really was or what he did. Ditto for the new girl, Myra...no, *Molly*.

There was no sense in changing his picture, since the one woman had already seen him—his body *all* fully fit and firm, he thought with a smug grin—and the other soon would. Still, there was no need to lay trouble on his doorstep. His grin widened. He'd *lay* that trouble elsewhere.

An hour later, he sat back, pleased with his changes. As Chad *Jensen*, he now "lived" in Waco. As a divorced—just in case he slipped up and mentioned his wife and kid sometime—marketing executive, he helped colleges recruit top athletes from across the nation, and he had to travel a lot. A traveling schedule would allow him to call the shots and juggle his women. The last thing he wanted was another female thinking she had a claim on him—or his time.

Before he logged off, he sent a message to Molly.

—I'm looking forward to meeting you next week, luv. Pleasant dreams.—

Chad powered off, not waiting for a response, since he wouldn't reply right away anyhow.

Better to play it slow—for now.

* * * *

"Yes, Mom, I know we haven't been down to see you." Angie put the cell on speaker phone so she could make sure Jessica's breakfast oatmeal got from her bowl to her mouth without half of it landing on the floor—or being splattered around the kitchen. "Chad's just been busy. It is football season, you know."

"It seems there's always something," her mother complained. "Austin is not that far away, and I'd like to see my grandchild before she graduates from high school."

"Jess is only two, Mother. I think you'll get the chance to see her in the next fifteen years."

"There's no need for sarcasm, Angelina."

Angie rolled her eyes, since she wasn't on Skype. Thank goodness her mother's knowledge of technology was limited and she didn't realize smart phones could activate that feature. Besides, if her mother saw her with no makeup and the oversized T-shirt that now sported oatmeal as well as spaghetti stains, she'd just be in for another lecture. "We'll try to get down soon. I promise."

"I suppose Thanksgiving is out?"

"Chad will be scouting games. Besides, you know you don't cook."

"There are plenty of restaurants that cater. What about Christmas?"

"You know as well as I do that Christmas is the Holy Grail of college ball. I won't even see Chad. I'll be lucky if he's even in Texas."

"Well, I think you make way too many sacrifices for that man. He needs to compromise and bring you and the baby down here. *Soon.*"

"Yes, Mom. Whoops, gotta go. Jess just knocked her bowl to the floor. Bye." Angie hung up, feeling a little guilty since her daughter was gazing at her with big, blue eyes and the bowl was still where it should be. But sometimes her mother got a little bit too close to the truth, and Angie was not about to share her concerns with anyone, least of all her mother, who had never liked Chad in the first place.

Angie set the bowl on the counter, wiped Jess's mouth with a napkin, and lifted her daughter out of the chair. As she followed the toddler into the living room, she told herself she really didn't have any serious marital problems. Coaches put in long hours. If they weren't working with their own team, they were out scouting the competition. Winning was everything. If they had a losing season, there might not be a job next year. She understood the stress, and she tried to be tolerant of the after-work happy hours. It wasn't as though Chad came home *drunk*.

Her conscience niggled at her as she sank onto the sofa. She should have stayed awake last night and waited for Chad to come to bed. When they first started dating and he still coached high school, they always had sex the night before a game. He said it brought him luck. She'd giggled secretly, since guys on the team had said the same thing, trying to persuade her and her friends when they were in high school—not that it had worked. Her father would have killed—or at least maimed—any boy who'd try. Of course, once she got to college, things had changed in that department.

Her sex life with Chad had subtly changed after they got married, but she supposed that was common since living with someone 24/7 wasn't the same as getting dressed up and going *out*. Who could look glam at seven o'clock in the morning anyhow?

More and more these days, too, Chad's coaching responsibilities had increased and "dates" no longer included evenings dancing. Instead, they were for sitting in the stands on Friday nights with the other coaches' wives while Chad was on the field. Saturdays were spent replaying—or as Chad called it, *analyzing*—the Friday night game with coaching staff, followed by *studying* college football plays.

All in all, it left precious little time to be involved with the folks she worked with at a local insurance company. Last year's Christmas party had been a disaster. Her boss, and just about everyone in the industry, was more concerned with health care reform than with which team would win the championship. Chad had sulked all the way home, claiming business needed to take an example from athletics.

"Mama! See me!"

Jessica had pulled her favorite doll from several lying in a recliner and was attempting to dance with it. Angie smiled at her daughter's antics, which amounted to jumping up and down. Tapping the music icon on her phone, Angie stood and held out her hand as her body began to move in rhythm to *Blurred Lines*.

God, she missed dancing.

****

Eve stopped at the pigeonholes that served as faculty mailboxes behind the front desk counter to check for mail on Monday morning. Since administrators had learned to function in the twenty-first century and use email, usually all she got were art catalogs and the occasional flyer advertising some art program. Still, as with snail-mail at home, it was fun to pick up actual pieces of mail, sort of like holding a real book rather than an e-reader. Next to her, Arthur Conrad, one of the history teachers, took a surprisingly large stack of papers out of his box and ruffled through them.

"You must not have picked up your mail in a while," Eve said.

He adjusted his reading glasses and smiled. "Actually, this is all recent."

"Really? How come so much?" The coaches' boxes were always crammed with sports stuff, but Arthur didn't coach.

"Debate materials," he answered. "The students have to build cases for both sides since they don't know whether they'll draw affirmative or negative arguments at the tournaments."

She should have remembered Arthur sponsored the debate team. He hardly looked like the argumentative type, though. His demeanor was always quiet and calm. A few inches taller than she, with a build more like a swimmer or cyclist than a jock, he wore his brown hair short and neatly trimmed. Even though she didn't think he was any older than she was, he always wore white shirts and ties rather than dressing casually.

"Your kids must be the only ones who like to study," Eve said.

He grinned, looking surprisingly boyish. "What kid doesn't like to argue?"

"That's true." Eve gathered her catalogs and stuffed them into her oversize bag. Nodding goodbye, she turned down the hall toward her room while Arthur went over to talk to Molly, the front desk clerk. She heard him say something about hoping she'd have a better Monday than last Friday.

Eve hoped he was right. Friday had been a mess for everyone. Worse, Brian hadn't come over for "dessert" at all. She had Blog-Faced him yesterday and gotten a short reply that he wouldn't be able to make it.

She truly was glad she didn't have kids of her own. After teaching all day, she didn't think she could go home and cope with more children, especially small ones. Chad had certainly increased his philandering since his daughter had been born, not that Eve could stand in judgment of him. Even in high school, cute girls had surrounded him and he'd had a super-inflated ego—which was one of the reasons they were friends and not lovers—and he expected his wife to adore him. Babies took time and energy, though. Eve had only met

Angelina once, at the same party where Brian had been introduced, and the girl had looked tired, but it really wasn't her business.

She flipped on her computer when she got to her room and checked the school's email. Faculty and staff were forbidden to use Blog-Face—or any other social media—on school computers, so what was there was mundane, at best. Faculty meeting after school on Tuesday, Parent-Teachers night on Thursday, and a message from one of the counselors to come to her office during planning time. Probably a new student enrolling. Deer Hill's policy was to give teachers as much background information as administration had on new students to help them fit in.

What Eve wasn't prepared for when she got to the counselor's office later was finding Brenda Caldwell waiting. What was Brian's wife doing here?

Chapter Three

Eve felt a flash of panic, much like she had when she'd smoked strong weed in college and there had been a knock on the dorm door. Her blood felt like ice in her veins. What was Brenda doing here? Had she somehow found out about the affair? Eve took a deep breath, steadying her nerves, and forced a smile as she nodded toward Brenda and then looked at Mrs. Smith, the counselor. "You wanted to see me?"

"Yes, please have a seat."

Surely, if Brian's wife were here to complain, there would be an administrator present? Counselors were support staff and had no authority over personnel matters. Not that Eve had done anything legally wrong. She hadn't messed with any students nor had she gotten involved with another faculty member, and she could certainly name some people who had done just that—

"Trey will be enrolling in your art class," the counselor was saying.

Eve frowned. Who in the heck was Trey? "I...I'm not sure I understand."

"Let me explain," Brenda said. "Trey is my son, and he got into quite a bit of trouble over the weekend. The police found marijuana in his friend's car when it was stopped for speeding after curfew. My husband had to do some very persuasive talking to keep Trey from going to Juvenile Hall with the rest of the group. My son obviously made a wrong choice in friends. I'm transferring him to Deer Hill to get him away from them."

So that explained why Eve hadn't seen Brian over the weekend. Had he ever told her his kids' names? She knew he had two, one in the military and the other still in school. She just hadn't ever expected to meet either one. And to have Trey in one of her classes? Was that a good thing or a bad thing? Had Brian agreed to it?

"I'm sorry to hear your son got into trouble," Eve said neutrally, "but if you and your husband feel a transfer is best, Deer Hill is a good school."

"Oh, my husband wants to send Trey away. I made the decision this morning that we will try this first."

So Brian didn't know?

"I was explaining to Mrs. Caldwell that we have an excellent student-led support group for students who take the pledge during Red Ribbon week to remain drug free." The counselor continued, beaming at Brenda as though all the world problems had just been solved. "And Red Ribbon week is coming up. Trey is arriving here just in time."

Eve studied the painting of some flowers in a vase on the wall. Support groups only worked if the person wanted to be a part of them. She'd tried one of those for spouses of gamblers for a while, foolishly hoping she could somehow reform her ex. She seriously doubted a kid who smoked pot over the weekend wanted to go to such a group, especially since there had been no major consequences for his behavior. Much better to have let him be taken to Juvie. It might have been an eye-opener.

Not her business.

Eve smiled. "Well, let's hope he will find the right

kind of friends here. What class period is he in?"

"First," the counselor answered. "Since that's past, you'll meet him tomorrow."

First period was Principles of Design. A pretty basic class, and most of the students in it were only there because they thought it was an easy elective—when they showed up, since it was so early. Eve hoped Brenda wasn't taking Trey out of the proverbial frying pan, but the counselor wouldn't take kindly to having her choice second-guessed. Eve stood. "I'm sure he will do fine."

Brenda rose also and frowned slightly. "You look familiar. Have we met?"

Another jolt of panic swept over her, but she managed to push it aside. She had met Brian in a perfectly acceptable social setting. She drew her brows together, as if trying to remember and then nodded. "I believe we were introduced at Metro U's coaches' dinner last Christmas. Chad Olsen is a long-time friend of mine."

"Ah, yes! I remember now. The baby was sick and Angie had to stay home. Chad told Brian, my husband, that you were his next best girl."

Trust Chad to say something like that. "We were in high school together, although I was a senior and he was a sophomore." A sophomore who dated senior girls.

"Did you meet my husband?"

Eve kept her face impassive, although it was a struggle. "Yes, Chad introduced us. He thinks quite highly of Mr. Caldwell."

Brenda smiled. "Brian hasn't quite gotten used to being called 'mister' instead of 'coach' yet, but I'm glad you met. It will be helpful to Trey that you know both of us."

Eve stifled the hysterical laughter attempting to bubble up in her throat.

How well Eve *knew* Brian would be her little secret.

Once back in her room, she whipped out her cell.

—Must see you. Can you come tonight?—

She had an instant response.

—I can *come* for you any night, babe. Sixish?—

Eve grinned and shook her head. Maybe it was better to soften the news with mind-blowing sex first.

Then she sobered, wondering what he'd say when he found out about Trey.

****

Molly looked around the lobby and the short corridor that led to the principal's office and hoped Mr. Conrad—Arthur, he had reminded her to call him that—was right. Today, even though it was a Monday, would be a better day than last Friday. Thank goodness the faculty at Deer Hill was friendly and supportive. It made dealing with irate parents tolerable. As Mr. Conrad—Arthur—had reminded her, a lot of parents these days had trouble handling their kids, so they were frustrated.

Case in point. A fashionably-dressed, platinum-haired woman had enrolled her sullen-looking son in school this morning. She had approached the front desk and inquired where the registrar's office was. Behind her back, the boy had rolled his eyes.

Molly felt sorry for the woman. Back home, kids showed respect to their parents, but maybe that was a product of small-town, rural life. Even the community college she'd attended nearby hadn't had major problems. Ironically, that was part of the reason Molly wanted to move to a big city. Not that she wanted problems. She just wanted to experience life on a larger scale.

Pulling her smart phone out of her handbag, she glanced at Blog-Face to see if Chad had sent another message. Nothing yet. He'd said he looked forward to meeting her this week…of course, this was only Monday. He had called her "luv" in the last message and she had loved it! It had a sweet '60s-era sound to it, meaning he'd remembered her telling him about loving British Retro. And Chad sounded sweet too. She could hardly wait to meet him.

Seeing Mrs. Wilson marching down the hall, radio in hand, a frown on her face, Molly tucked the cell phone away. "I wonder what's wrong now."

"Hard to say," Irma Torres, one of the English teachers who'd come up behind her, answered. "I hope it isn't that new student I got this morning. He sure wasn't happy to be here."

"I know." Molly felt another wave of sympathy for the mother. "Maybe he's new to the area and didn't like leaving his friends."

"You have the part of leaving his friends right," the English teacher said. "but the family lives in Dallas. His dad is the athletic director at Metro U. and the mother is on a host of charity boards."

"She seemed nice," Molly replied. "Hopefully, her son will fit in and make some new friends."

"Maybe. He's got Arthur Conrad for history, who'll keep an eye on him, and Eve O'Connor for art. She tries to get the kids to be creative."

As the teacher left, Molly thought about Eve O'Connor. In contrast to Mr. Conrad—Arthur—who was always upbeat, Eve seemed somewhat bitter, although she was always friendly enough. She just didn't seem happy. Molly knew Eve was divorced. Did she sit at home alone on Friday nights too?

Her cell dinged, and she pulled it out for a quick look. Chad! He'd sent a message!

—Hello, Luv. Would you like to meet at the Pendulum for a drink on Wednesday around five o'clock?—

The Pendulum! She'd heard of the place close to the West End. It was a Retro-bar, named after the old hit song, *England Swings*. Choosing that bar to meet just showed how kind and considerate Chad was!

Quickly, she responded.

—I would absolutely "luv" it!—

Molly smiled, feeling a delightful shiver slide down her spine. If all went well, maybe she wouldn't be sitting home alone on this Friday night.

****

Eve tossed her head, clearing the long strands of hair from her face. "Ummm. Yes! That's it." Her outstretched hands clung to the bedpost in her apartment as she gave Brian better access. "Go deeper!"

He grunted, thrusting harder and faster, one arm clasped around her while his other hand kneaded a breast, fingers pulling forcefully on the taut tip, eliciting groans of pleasure from deep within her.

Eve watched Brian in the reflection of the full-length mirror on the opposite wall.

They were both naked, but leaning over her as he was, the width of his shoulders seemed broader and the bulk of his biceps larger, an altogether most pleasing image. She arched her back, and expertly, he teased her until she erupted like a geyser that had been simmering just beneath the earth's surface.

"Christ, you're going to kill me," Brian said as they both collapsed on the bed, bodies slippery with sweat. "I'm not a college kid anymore."

Eve rolled on her side, letting her fingers slide the length of his organ, which jerked at her touch. "No? Seems the Big Guy might disagree with you."

He laughed. "You're the one who makes the Big Guy react like a kid."

Eve smiled and sat up before Brian could pull her back for another session.

"Christ," he said again. "Now you're going to make me wait for next time?"

"Yes," she said, standing and reaching for her clothes. "You know this was just supposed to be a quickie to make up for the weekend. You need to get home for dinner."

"I've already had you for dinner," he growled, retrieving his clothes from a heap on the floor. "I just want seconds."

"Well, so do I, but you really don't have time. Besides I Blog-Faced you for a reason today."

He frowned as he put on his shirt. "Yeah, I forgot there was another reason for my coming over. What is it?"

Eve paused and then zipped her jeans. "Your wife was at Deer Hill today."

His hand stilled on his own zipper, his face paling beneath his tan. "Why?"

"It's not what you think," Eve said quickly. "She doesn't know anything about us. She was there to enroll your son, Trey."

"Trey? After what happened this weekend—I assume you know?—I told her I was sending him off to a boot camp west of Fort Worth for the rest of the semester."

"She obviously didn't agree with you."

His jaw clenched. "That's always been part of the problem."

"Well, I'm not getting in the middle of that," Eve said, "but I wanted you to know he'll be attending Deer Hill."

"It's a big school. You probably won't even run into him."

"Actually, I'll be running into him tomorrow," Eve said. "That was the other thing I wanted to tell you. Trey has been enrolled in my art class."

Brian's expression of incredulous shock would have been comical except the subject was serious.

"*What*?"

"Do you really need for me to repeat it?"

His dazed look faded as he clenched his jaw. "No. What the hell possessed Brenda to enroll Trey in *art* class, for God's sake?"

Eve arched a brow. "Studies have shown that fine arts give some troubled kids an outlet for creativity which keeps them out of trouble."

He shook his head. "Ah, you know I didn't mean it like that. Athletics gives kids the same opportunity. Trey's never cared for either. He's turning into a problem kid."

"Trust me. I deal with lots of problem kids." Eve paused. "You do trust me? He'll never find out about us."

"Trust isn't the point. I just don't want you to have to deal with him."

"Don't worry about that." Eve frowned. "He wasn't enrolled in an art class at his old school?"

"The closest thing to art was a tech-graphics class. He got kicked out of it when his teacher found him trying to hack into the school's notification system to parents." Brian suddenly looked hopeful. "Deer Hill must have something like that. Can't you get his schedule changed?"

"Changing his schedule, especially since he hasn't even attended my class, would only arouse suspicions." She glanced at Brian, hoping the little *entendre* would ease his tension, but he missed it completely. "Anyway, Trey's records would have been sent over. If he got caught hacking, admin won't allow him to take any kind of tech course. That's probably why the counselor put him in my art class."

Brian nodded glumly. "Well, keep me informed."

"I will." Eve hesitated. "I'll also have to keep your wife informed since she's the one who enrolled Trey. She might question if I suddenly made you the contact."

"I suppose you're right." Brian pulled Eve into his arms. "Are you sure you can handle this?"

She smiled and rose on tiptoe to nibble his ear. "I think the real question is, can you handle me?"

His hands slid up to knead her breasts. "Let's find out."

****

That last round of sex with Eve had made him really late getting home, but Brian was still angry enough at Brenda for taking matters into her own hands that he didn't care. What was even worse was Eve had to work him—really *work* him—to get him to come. Hellfire and damnation! He'd never had any problem in that area.

His wife was waiting for him in the parlor, wine glass in hand. He hated the parlor, decorated as it was with sheer curtains, flowery wallpaper, and fancy ceramic figurines on every table. The ivory satin, fancy-legged Queen Isabel—or Anne or someone—chairs looked too spindly for a man to sit on. The small sofa—*chaise*, Brenda called it—wasn't much better, upholstered in rose silk. The room always made him feel like a wild boar who'd dug under the wrong fence to find himself cornered.

Looking elegant and at ease, his wife perched on the sofa in black hostess trousers and a cream-colored blouse with tiny pearl buttons—the kind that always made him want to rip them away.

Brenda had chosen her battleground well.

Brian took a deep, steadying breath. He hadn't been a winning coach for years without recognizing strategy when he saw it. If she thought to have him at a disadvantage through her choice of location, she could think again. A good offense was the best defense.

"I had a call from Deer Hill High School today," he said as he entered the room and went straight to the small bar trolley and poured himself a Scotch. "You enrolled *our* son there without discussing it with me."

Her eyes flickered, but she remained composed. "I did not want Trey staying home, sleeping until noon, thinking he was on vacation."

"We were talking about boot camp, the last I heard."

"*You* were talking about boot camp. Sending Trey off to a boys' camp run by religious fanatics is not the answer."

"They aren't religious fanatics. They're ex-military special ops. The program is *just* what Trey needs. Getting kicked out of that tech class was bad enough, but messing with drugs? You want an addict living here?"

"They had one marijuana cigarette. You are over-reacting. It wasn't like they were doing hard drugs or trying to sell anything."

Brian stared at her, wondering if serving on all her charity committees had put her mind in some kind of ivory tower lockup. "How do you know it was just one joint? Where did they get it? Drug dealers aren't exactly pillars of the community."

"Trey said his friend John got it from another friend in gym class."

"And you believed him?"

"Of course. Why wouldn't I? He's our son."

Brian slammed his empty glass down hard enough to make Brenda wince. At least he was getting some kind of reaction out of her. "Kids who sneak out after curfew, get caught speeding, with *drugs,* are also probably prone to *lying.* Or had that thought not occurred to you?"

This time she flinched. He knew he was being harsh, but damn it! Trey was his son too. "This isn't the same as a kid pilfering a candy bar off the rack."

"I know that. I am not stupid." Her hand trembled slightly as she put her wine glass down on the table. "I just want him to have a chance at another school before we take harsher measures. I talked with each teacher today. They were all supportive and they all agreed to stay in touch with me."

Brian's thoughts flew to Eve as he'd left her, lying naked on her black satin sheets, her long, red hair tousled and spread across the pillow like hot lava. He was having trouble aligning that image with "school teacher," let alone one who would be in continual contact with his wife.

Hell, what was he getting himself into?

Chapter Four

Eve did a quick survey of her first period class Tuesday morning, but except for the usual tardy students trailing in, she didn't spot anyone new. She hoped Trey would show. She did not want to have to call Brian's wife because their son was truant the first day.

She really didn't want to talk to Brenda at all. Knowing Brian had a wife was one thing. Eve had, after all, deliberately chosen to have an affair with a married man because he would be safe from commitment and she wouldn't be subject to having her savings taken from her again. Getting to *know* the wife was another thing altogether.

They certainly weren't going to be one big, happy family. On the other hand, Eve had no desire to deceive the woman, either.

"All right, class," Eve said as she turned on the Power Point and motioned for a student to turn off the lights, "let's take a look at how line and space define composition."

The massive grumbling at having to take out notebooks halted abruptly. Eve looked up from the computer to see what had caused the sudden silence and then followed her students' gazes toward the doorway.

In the dim light from the projector's beam, it seemed like a dark specter in a cape loomed in the doorway. Her first thought was that one of her students decided to dress up early for Halloween, even though costumes weren't allowed. When the tall, lanky figure moved away from the doorframe, Eve realized it must be Trey.

As he moved inside the classroom, she recognized the cape as a long, black coat, worn open, which caused it to flap. Beneath it, Trey wore a black T-shirt and black jeans. His inky hair reached his shoulders, and when he moved closer, she saw his eyes were nearly as dark. He looked completely Goth, although she thought that style had disappeared a while back.

Handing her his admission slip silently, he turned to stare at the class, a challenging look on his face. One of her soccer players obviously recognized the look, for his jaw jutted out and he began to rise.

Hoping to avoid a confrontation—good God, kids got upset over nothing—Eve spoke quickly. "Students, this is Trey, who is new to Deer Hill. Since this is first period, it would be helpful if someone will help Trey get acquainted with the building today." She leveled a stern look at Bob, the soccer player. "I believe your coach mentioned you had some detention hours to make up? Perhaps if you could escort Trey around, those hours could be waived."

Bob frowned and slid back into his seat. "Yeah, sure."

Eve ignored his less-than-enthusiastic response and pointed to an empty chair toward the back. "Why don't you sit there for today, Trey?"

He stared at Bob a few seconds longer and then shrugged. "Yeah, sure."

As he moved to his seat, Eve switched to the first slide, beginning an explanation on different types of lines.

The crisis had been averted, at least for now, but she sensed trouble brewing.

****

"You're certainly dressed up," Joni said to Molly the next morning as they took their places by the front desk counter. "Any reason?"

"I've got a date tonight. Well, this afternoon. After work."

"The cute guy you met on Blog-Face?"

Molly felt herself blush. "Yes, he seems really nice."

"So where are you going?"

"The Pendulum. I told Chad about my love for British Retro, and he picked the pub. Isn't that considerate of him?"

"Sounds like it. You'll have to fill me in tomorrow."

"Okay." Molly looked at her friend. Joni was a few years older than her, and divorced. She dated around. "You don't think I'm dressed too brazenly, do you? "

"Brazenly? I'm not sure what that word means, but if you mean sexy, no."

"The neckline isn't too low?"

Joni laughed. "Honey, have you looked at what our female students wear? Half their boobs hang out most of the time."

"I don't want to give the wrong impression on a first date." Molly started to tell Joni that she'd spent most of last night trying on and discarding nearly everything she owned before deciding on a cotton peasant blouse with lace sleeves and a scooped neckline, coupled with a flowery gauze skirt, but decided Joni would just think her silly.

But it had been an agonizing decision. Molly knew she wasn't the chic type like the platinum-blonde lady who'd enrolled her son Monday, and she wasn't the sexy, curvaceous type like Miss O'Connor. Nor did she have the avant-garde style of tall, skinny models with long, straight hair and smoldering eyes. Her own figure was slightly plump. Her brown hair curled in an unruly way, giving her more of an Annie look—minus the freckles—than anything else, although her mother always said her hazel eyes were pretty. Molly didn't want to look too refreshing. The outfit she'd chosen made her feel a little daring, like a Folklorico dancer she'd seen once at a fair.

She just hoped Chad would like it.

****

Chad arrived ten minutes early at the pub. Some guys liked to arrive a little late so they didn't give the impression of being too eager, but he'd learned women responded a lot better—and more quickly to bed—if he was waiting. Besides, it gave him an opportunity to scope out the place, in case the date didn't work out.

The bartender had just set down his beer when Molly Whitefield appeared outside the glass door to the bar. She hesitated and glanced around. Chad wondered if she'd suddenly changed her mind or if she expected him to be on the sidewalk waiting. She took a deep breath. Was she nervous? How interesting. Most of the women he connected with on Blog-Face were seasoned bar flirts. Molly pushed the door open and stepped inside.

He stood immediately, playing the courteous gentleman, and waved. Her look of relief was almost comic as she hurried over to him, as though the inside of a bar was foreign territory. Come to think of it, she did look a little out of place, given the country look of what she wore. He could almost picture her sitting on a hay bale in a barn with a couple of cows lowing in stalls. Even better, scatter the hay in an empty stall and tug that blouse off her shoulders where it should be…

"Chad?" she asked as if she weren't quite sure.

"Yes. I'm assuming you're Molly?" He smiled and pulled out a chair by the table for her to sit down, signaling a waitress. "What will you have?"

"A white wine spritzer, please."

She wasn't much of a drinker if she added seltzer water to wine. That wasn't necessarily a bad thing. Drunk women weren't that great in bed. The order was in keeping with that fresh country-girl look she had. Was she playing a part? He liked scenarios. Most of the time they involved something with bondage and spanking, but he could do variety. If she wanted to act the farmer's daughter, he could well play the traveling salesman. He grinned inwardly. "Traveling salesman" was close to what his profile claimed anyway. "I'm glad you could join me."

"I'm glad you invited me," Molly replied and looked around the room, wide-eyed. "Oh, my gosh! This looks just like how I imagined an English pub would look. Dark wood and gnarled tables and concrete floors! They've even got a copy of the lyrics to *England Swings* on the wall. And the posters! Beatles. Stones. Dave Clark Five. Herman's Hermits. My gran owns all those records! She'd love this place!"

"Was she English?"

Molly giggled. "No. Gran was in high school when Ed Sullivan put them all on TV. She and her friends started using English accents, much to their history teacher's chagrin. Grandpa has one of those shirts that says, 'I may be old, but I got to see all the great bands.' Of course, my great-grandfather argues that the Big Bands of the forties were better." She stopped, putting a hand to her mouth. "I'm talking too much. I always do when I'm nervous."

"There's no reason to be nervous." Chad smiled and took her hand, wondering if she'd pull it away. When she didn't, he lightly brushed his thumb across her knuckles. She stared at their hands as if they were strange objects. Either she was really good at role-playing or…could she actually be that innocent? "Where do your parents live?" he asked as he released her hand.

Her gaze returned to his face, her expression guileless. "Calle Verde, a little town in the Hill Country. Daddy and Grandpa operate a vineyard, and Gran does crafts for a store in Fredericksburg—" Molly stopped again, blushing. "I am definitely talking way too much."

"No you aren't. Go on."

"Are you sure? You've hardly been able to get a word in. I want to know all about you."

"The information will keep. Please, continue."

As she chattered on about small-town life and wanting to get to Big D, Chad found himself strangely intrigued. His common sense told him this situation would never work, especially since she'd told him she worked at Deer Hill. Eve would give him hell if she ever found out he was messing around with someone she knew.

Molly had neither sophistication nor worldly experience. She'd probably expect a relationship. Hell, he knew she would. He should cut his losses, fold his cards, finish the drink, and make an excuse to leave. He liked sultry, cosmopolitan women, not naïve, ingenuous girls.

But…what if she really were as artless as she sounded? She said she was twenty-two. Could anyone that age still be innocent? Or maybe even a virgin?

The thought hit him like a linebacker's tackle. He'd never had a virgin. Even in high school, he'd dated older girls who'd taught him tricks. Angie certainly had been around the block a few times before they screwed. Hell, a virgin? Was it possible?

"Let's have another drink," Chad said.

****

Molly was almost late to work on Thursday. Mrs. Wilson stood like a sentry at the front door, telling students to hurry up or they'd be tardy to class. She glanced at her wristwatch as Molly hurried up the steps.

"I'm sorry. I forgot to set the alarm," Molly said. "It won't happen again."

The principal didn't answer, just gave her a tight-lipped nod, and Molly thought it better not to pursue further conversation. Besides, she had a headache and her stomach was queasy. All she wanted this morning was coffee, and she hadn't even had time for that.

"You look a little peaked," Joni said when Molly tossed her bag down and quickly sat. "Late night with the new guy?"

"No. I was home by eight. It was just drinks."

Joni raised a brow. "Three hours is a long time for drinks. How many did you have anyway?"

"Three. I think. Maybe four. We were talking, and I kind of lost track."

"Four? Did you eat?"

Molly shook her head. "We were talking."

"Well, girl, I'd say that green tinge to your face is a

hangover."

"A hangover?"

"Yeah, you know, when you drink too much and don't eat."

"I know what a hangover is," Molly said, her stomach beginning to roil. "I just don't get them since I don't drink a lot."

"You've got one now." Joni rummaged in her desk and drew out a roll of peppermints. "Here. Take one. It'll settle your stomach."

"How did you know—"

"Been there. Done that."

Surprisingly, the mint did help. Plus, it got rid of the bitter taste in her mouth that lingered even after she'd brushed her teeth this morning. Had she really gotten drunk? She remembered Chad had ordered several drinks, but he'd assured her watered-down wine didn't have much effect. And she didn't think it had, except to make her feel like an urban woman, capable of holding the interest of a man who looked like he belonged on the cover of a romance novel.

Chad's attention had been focused on *her,* in spite of the number of scantily clad girls who kept walking by their table. He had paid them no mind, continuing to hold her hand—the one that didn't have the wine glass in it— and sending hot little shivers up her arm from the gentle caressing of his thumb on her palm. How could such a utilitarian appendage be so sexy? Chad had made her feel sexy, too, another experience she hadn't had before. Tommy had not ever stirred her blood or caused her to desire anything more than just a good-night peck on the cheek. And Molly had wanted Chad to kiss her. Really kiss her.

Her cheeks warmed, remembering how she'd stumbled against him as they left the bar. He'd taken her arm to steady her and considerately asked if she was all right. He'd walked her to her car to make sure she was safe, making her feel like a lady with her very own knight. He'd also made sure her seatbelt was fastened, after which he'd leaned down to her open window and traced his finger along her cheek in the lightest of feather strokes. And then, he'd brushed his lips over her mouth in the lightest of kisses.

"Check Blog-Face when you get home," he said.

A message had been waiting.

—Let me know when you get home. Sweet Dreams.—

How gallant, like a knight of olden times concerned for his lady. Emboldened by the wine, she had dared to answer.

—My dreams will be of you.—

And his answer:

—I hope I'm naked.—

Molly's face had heated at the images that message had conjured, and she'd been emboldened enough to reply.

—I'll let you know.—

Her cheeks flamed, thinking of his response.

—Looking forward to that.—

Joni gave her a curious look. "Are you all right? Your face just went from green to red like a stop light."

"I'm fine." Suddenly the headache was gone. She was so much more than fine! Molly was pretty sure she just might be falling in love with the perfect guy.

****

Eve tossed a bunch of junk mail from her teacher

box into the trash and watched Molly rush down the hall to the restrooms the next morning.

"Is she okay?" Eve asked Joni.

"Just an extended happy hour last night. She's not used to drinking."

"Poor kid. Middle-of-the-week hangovers are tough."

Joni grinned. "Yeah, but she said it was worth it. She finally met the guy who'd been flirting with her on Blog-Face."

Eve grimaced. Blog-Face hadn't been around ten years ago when she met her dead-beat husband, but dating on-line sure had. What an idiot she had been to fall for everything he said. "Tell her to be careful. Who knows who these guys really are."

"I told her. She met him at the Pendulum. According to Molly, he's Sir Galahad, Prince Charming, and Thor all in one body."

Eve laughed. "He must really be something to see. Still, make sure she wears real glasses, not rose-colored ones. At least half of what's said on Blog-Face is blarney."

"Yeah, I know. I've had a few encounters with guys who were less than truthful, let alone looking nothing like their pictures! I guess this one measured up, though."

"Looks can be deceiving."

"True. Speaking of looks, how is that new kid doing? The one who looks like a young, brooding Heathcliff dressed all in black."

"Heathcliff?" Eve shook her head. "I think you ladies spend way too much time reading romances. So far, though, there hasn't been any trouble."

Yet, she thought as she walked back to her room. *Not yet.*

Chapter Five

"Yes. The fundraiser is set to kick off Saturday morning, rain or shine," Brenda said to the president of the Junior League as she poured freshly brewed Columbian coffee into a delicate, gold-rimmed cup. Setting the phone to speaker, Brenda continued folding her egg-white omelette in one pan and turned the low-fat bacon slices over in another. "I have everything under control," she added as she checked the whole-wheat toast and took a china plate from the cabinet. "Yes. Yes. Don't worry."

Brenda disconnected, wishing she could convince Julia, the president, that the pledges she'd received would be honored regardless of whether every walker showed up to do the 5K or not. Proceeds were going toward a children's hospital wing, and the donors were all too political-minded to renege on pledges after their names had been published in the *Dallas Morning News*. Once the patrons' names were published, collecting the donations was a *fait accompli*. She had done so many of these things, it was practically child's play.

Grating fresh parmesan onto her eggs, Brenda added the toast and bacon and carried the plate to the dining room, stopping in the doorway to admire the setting. The cream color of the damask wallpaper lent an elegant look to the windowless room. A snowy white tablecloth covered the mahogany table that sat twelve. Polished silver gleamed in the light of a massive chandelier whose light also glinted off the Waterford crystal holding her hand-squeezed juice. Sipping her coffee, Brenda sat down to savor her meal.

Breakfast was her favorite time of day. The house was peaceful and quiet, and the business of the day had not yet begun. Brian always left early, grabbing an unhealthy breakfast taco from God-knows-where, and Trey met his friends at McDonalds.

Or she thought that was what he had been doing.

Brenda hoped she'd done the right thing with Trey. Tomorrow was the end of his first week at Deer Hill, and she'd called the counselor to set up meeting times with the teachers. She hoped the news would be encouraging. At least, none of them had called her yet.

Even before Saturday night's incident with the police, she'd decided Trey needed a different school. Having been dropped from the tech class because of alleged hacking—did Trey actually know how to do that?—was a huge blemish to his reputation. Maybe the defamation had even led to his trying that marijuana cigarette.

She'd known Brian would be angry about her decision, which was why she'd dressed rather provocatively at the dinner and allowed him to do whatever he wanted to her in bed. Sex usually worked, but this time it hadn't.

Brian's way to deal with a problem was to tackle it straight on, bulldozing through any obstacles to achieve his outcome. The problem was that their son was not a football and his life wasn't a hundred-yard run for a touchdown. Sometimes, Brenda wondered if Brian's brain had been connected to athletics for too long. He still lived and breathed sports, even though he'd been promoted to Athletic Director from the coaching staff, a feat she'd had a small part in making sure happened. Not that he'd find out.

Brenda took a bite of egg, savoring the fluffiness of her endeavor. Most omelettes were heavy and flat, but she had learned to fast-whip air into the mix and cover it at the last minute so it would puff up like a soufflé. A touch of coarse pepper was the perfect complement to the cheese, and the whole thing was healthy. It truly was too bad neither her husband nor her son saw the sense in eating right, but in her discussion with other ladies on the many committees on which she served, men not eating healthy seemed to be a universal problem.

Right now, her immediate concern was Trey's success at the new school. Perhaps, in a new environment, she could even convince him to cut his hair and quit wearing all those black clothes. Maybe the school even had a dress code that she could use in her persuasion.

And, of course, she'd enlist the help of his teachers, beginning by finding out what their personal interests were. In her opinion, such knowledge went a long way in persuasion.

****

"All right, class. That was the tardy bell. Stash all the electronics." Eve kept her eyes on her desktop, taking roll. She'd found it easier to get the kids actually to put away the phones and tabs if she didn't look at them directly when she said it. They probably saw it as less of a personal challenge, she supposed. At any rate, it didn't give them the opportunity to argue.

She stood, noticing two girls in the back of the room

with thumbs still busily engaged. "Ten seconds to wrap that up or you'll have to pick up your phones at the end of the day."

"Just one more sentence," one said.

"I have to check a message," the other added.

"Ah, come on, Miss O'Connor. Don't you use Blog-Face?" someone asked.

"Yes, I do, but I'm not addicted to it." Eve shook her head. "The world's not going to end if you miss a Blog-Face post."

"What if we miss a notification that the Zombie Apocalypse has begun?"

Eve looked at the boy who'd called out, wishing she could respond with something suitable, like maybe she already had a roomful of zombies, since they weren't interested in learning much. But Mrs. Wilson would have a coronary if, heaven forbid, a teacher was sarcastic. "If that happens, I'm sure it will be announced over the P.A."

Some of the class laughed, which proved at least some of them were actually listening. Trey just looked at her and smiled slightly.

It was the same kind of half-smile he'd given her the past three days when she'd made some off-the-wall comment. Part-smirk, as if he recognized some hidden meaning behind her words, but his eyes didn't smile. Instead, his dark gaze remained trained on her, as though she were an interesting specimen under a microscope. He'd made no personal remarks. In fact, he'd rarely spoken at all, but whenever she looked at him, he was watching. Eve supposed she should be grateful that at least one student paid attention, but the feeling was unsettling.

The fact that Trey looked so much like his father didn't help either. Although Brian's hair was neatly trimmed and had touches of silver in the black, the other features—straight nose, full mouth, and firm jaw—were obvious. Only the eyes were different. Brian's were a deep, velvety brown, the faint laugh-lines at the corners indicating a man who enjoyed living life. Trey's were nearly obsidian, his look practically as hard as the volcanic glass itself. Eve hoped he didn't have an explosive nature beneath that quiet, steady demeanor he showed.

She wondered if he'd made any friends yet. She'd hoped Bob, who was really a pretty good kid, would befriend Trey after showing him around, but they'd ignored each other after that first day. Being a loner wasn't good.

Eve sighed. She'd hoped to keep herself separated from Brian's private life—particularly from his wife—but with Trey in her class now, she needed to know what made him tick. And the best person to ask was his mother.

****

"So far, the reports on Trey have been fairly good," Brenda said the next afternoon when Eve arrived at the counselor's office for their conference. "I hope you've not had problems?"

"He's not been disruptive," Eve replied, wondering how she could bring up the uneasy feeling she had about Trey without sounding like she thought he had a mental problem. Parents never wanted to hear that anything might be wrong. "In fact, he's very quiet, but perhaps it's because he hasn't had time to make new friends yet."

"We—my husband and I—have cautioned Trey not

to make new friends too quickly, given how his former friends turned out. We certainly don't want Trey getting mixed up with the wrong crowd." Brenda smoothed a slight wrinkle from her pencil skirt and turned to the counselor. "Is there a big drug problem at Deer Hill?"

"No," the counselor answered and then pursed her mouth when Eve raised a questioning eyebrow. "That is, not a huge problem. There are a few individuals who break the rules."

Eve arched her brow a bit further. Mrs. Smith seemed to be forgetting that just last Friday, a whole section of bleachers had reeked of weed. But then, maybe Mrs. Smith didn't know what marijuana smelled like. She was well past retirement age, and Eve doubted the woman had taken part in the Hippie movement. Besides, she stayed in her office as much as possible.

"It's good to be cautious," Eve agreed, "but I don't want your son to feel alienated, either. A new school can be difficult to adjust to. Are there any extracurricular activities he would like to join?"

"He was in a technology club at his old school. Trey loves computers. He practically lives on Blog-Face, but then, I guess every teenager does."

"Unfortunately, true," Eve said. "I sometimes wonder if society is losing its ability to have actual face-to-face conversations."

Brenda laughed. "That is exactly what my husband said not long ago, but then, Brian is the sort of man who likes to interact."

Eve started, hoping her face hadn't turned red. If only Brenda knew just how much her husband liked to *interact*. In spite of where she was, her body started to tingle as she remembered his hands gliding over her nude body. Good Lord. This was not the time to be thinking about *that*. "Ummm…I remember my friend, Chad, telling me your husband is the athletic director at Metro U. I'm surprised Trey isn't playing sports."

Brenda shrugged a slender, cashmere-covered shoulder. "Brian has tried. There were pitched battles before each sport season in middle school, but Trey prefers computer games to the field."

Which Brian would see as defiance. It wasn't Eve's business, but she couldn't help asking, "Trey simply refused?"

"In a manner of speaking. I supported his…decision, I guess you could call it. Football is such a violent game, and I didn't want Trey to get hurt."

Eve's mouth almost dropped, but she managed to keep it closed. How could anyone be married to a coach—especially one who was an athletic director, and not take an interest in sports? Angie had attended all of Chad's games when he coached high school and even some of the college games before Jessica came along. Not that her actions had kept Chad corralled, but still—

"Well, enough about us for the moment," Brenda said. "I always like to know something about Trey's teachers. Do you mind?"

"Of course not," Eve replied. She generally gave background information to parents at the fall Open House anyway. "I'm a native Texan, raised in Austin. I graduated from UT with a major in art and a minor in English. After graduation, I moved to Dallas. I've been teaching at Deer Hill for ten years."

"Do you have children?"

A loaded question. Parents seemed to think an adult couldn't relate to their kids if the adult didn't have children of her own. When Eve replied no, subtle—and sometimes not so subtle—questions were asked, and Eve did not wish to discuss her wretched marriage or her wretched jerk of an ex-husband, so she used a white lie.

"I am unable to have children," Eve replied. It really wasn't a *big* lie, since the pill rendered her incapable of reproducing. She quickly transitioned the conversation. "On the other hand, I suppose you could say I have a hundred and fifty children, since I see them every day. I feel quite blessed with my life." Eve had learned adding that last bit, even though it was a bit hypocritical, seemed to silence the do-gooders who wanted to express unwanted sympathy or talk about adoption options.

Brenda looked as though she were trying to frown, and Eve realized the woman must have had Botox, since her forehead was not moving. She hoped the treatment would evolve by the time she needed it done. Had Brenda had other work?

"I didn't mean to bring up an indelicate subject. Of course, couples can be very happy without children."

Mrs. Smith lowered her glasses and looked over them at Eve. "Didn't you get a divorce last year?"

Good God. Trust the elderly counselor to remember that bit of gossip. Eve forced a smile. "Yes, I did."

"So that was the problem? Oh, you poor dear. We thought—"

Eve knew exactly what everyone had thought. The divorce had been sudden. As soon as Eve realized her ex had emptied her savings account, she'd called a lawyer friend. Forty-eight hours later, the papers had been served and door locks changed. Everyone thought there'd been another woman involved, which was almost amusing to Eve now, given her present circumstances, but it had seemed a better excuse than acknowledging she'd been too stupid to realize her husband was a compulsive gambler.

"I am so sorry! I truly did not mean to pry," Brenda said as she stood. "I really must be going."

Eve stood as well. Discussing Trey's unsettling behavior would have to wait. "I must go too," she said, since Mrs. Smith was assuming the maternal, grandmotherly look she used with students. "I have a class in a few minutes."

Once safely back in her room, Eve took out her cell and clicked on Blog-Face. She had given Brenda no reason to suspect she was even interested in another man, let alone a married one, but better to let Brian know the way the conversation had gone.

—Can we talk tonight?—

—Sure, babe. Sex first?—

—When don't we?—

—Then I can count on *after* too?—

—Sex demon.—

—Seductress.—

—I'll wear red.—

—Not for long.—

—We'll see. *Slàinte.*—

—Are you going Irish on me?—

—Aye. It means "good health"—you're going to need it!—

—Are you questioning my stamina?—

—Never.—

Eve smiled as she clicked off the site. Red was his favorite color. Brian made her feel as young as that new front desk clerk, albeit with probably more experience. And Brian was a man with a slow hand—which was all she needed.

****

"You seem distracted tonight," Brian said as he slid himself out of Eve and rolled on his side, pushing the tangled sheets away and propping his head on his hand.

"I'm sorry," Eve replied as she reached down to fondle him. "I'll make it up to you."

Brian caught her hand and folded it in his. "Not important. What's the matter?"

Eve sighed. "I don't know exactly. Probably nothing more than ordinary, everyday stress from school."

"Does this have something to do with my wife?" Brian's dark brown eyes gazed into Eve's. "She said she was going to the school today. Did she upset you?"

"No. She was very nice."

"She didn't ask any prying questions?"

"Not really. She asked if I had children, but that's a fairly common question from parents. Why do you ask?"

"Brenda is a strategist. She analyzes people. Sizes them up to see where they might fit in her grand scheme of things."

Eve knit her brows, puzzled. "Why would she do that to me? I'm an elective teacher that Trey got stuck with."

"Doesn't matter if you're a teacher, counselor, whatever. Anyone who has contact with Trey is important. When it comes to him, Brenda is like a she-bear."

"But she won't recognize he has problems?"

"Nope. She rationalizes that someone else is at fault. Trey was just in the wrong place at the wrong time. The kid figured out long ago how to use that to his advantage. Whenever he didn't want to do something I told him to do, he'd take his version of whatever it was to his mother, and she'd defend him."

"Kids have been playing one parent against the other for millennia. I see it all the time," Eve said, noncommittal in tone. The conversation was really going in a direction she wasn't sure she wanted to take.

"He's not a child anymore. He needs to take responsibility for his actions. He's going to be eighteen soon. The next time he gets stopped by the police, I won't be able to bail him out."

"I wish I could help. I mean, I'll try to help, but I—we—are walking a fine line here. If I get too involved, your wife might get suspicious. She knows we met at the Christmas party last year, but I don't think she has made any connection."

"Doubtful. She's accustomed to my being out. Half the time, she is too, with one charity function or another. What she's focusing on right now is Trey."

"That's not a totally bad thing."

"Maybe not. I still think the kid needs boot camp."

"So far, he's not been a behavior problem."

"He shouldn't be, since he's the one who chose Deer Hill—or at least, he did once he realized he wasn't going to be allowed to drop out."

"Why would he choose Deer Hill?"

Brian shrugged. "He gave Brenda some rubbish about it had a website-building class he'd found on-line."

Eve sat up and hugged a pillow. "That's a popular class. All in all, Deer Hill is a good school. We have high test scores, in spite of the fact that most of the time the kids seem apathetic."

Brian tugged the pillow away and tossed it aside. "I like seeing you naked, babe, even when we're talking. I know Deer Hill is good. Brenda would never have allowed Trey to attend a school that wasn't. My concern is if he knows kids from here that might be into drugs."

"You don't think last weekend was a one-time incident?"

Brian snorted. "Brenda may be in denial, but I'm not. I'd bet a month's salary getting that joint from a friend in gym class was no accident. I'd bet another month that it wasn't the first time, either."

"Trey hasn't connected with anyone that I know of. He kind of stays to himself, even at lunch."

"That's some stupid phase he's going through, like dressing all in black. The friends he hung out with considered themselves to be "intellectually inclined" as he told me last year when I tried to persuade him once more to try out for some sport."

"The aloof, superior attitude is part of the Goth thing. We used to have a group of them at school. They tended to be a bit dramatic—given to dismissive looks and long sighs at having to follow rules they considered oppressive." Eve grinned. "But then, what teenager doesn't feel like the whole world of adults exists only to curb their fun?"

"You got that right, babe."

"Here's something else I've got right," Eve replied as she leaned over and brushed her nipples against Brian's bare chest and then nibbled his ear. "Adults do exist for something else."

"Oh, yeah." In one adept move, Brian flipped Eve onto her back and straddled her. "Playtime."

Chapter Six

"At least, you won Saturday," Eve told Chad the next Tuesday afternoon as they met in their favorite bar.

"By a field goal. Dunster's not happy."

Eve popped the olive from her martini into her mouth. "A win is a win. Why do head coaches always think they have to slaughter the opposition? Football isn't war."

Chad scowled. "Each game is a battle. The other team is the enemy, as far as we're concerned."

"Whatever happened to sportsmanship?"

"It went the way of bipartisanship in Congress." Chad finished his beer and signaled for another. "A weak team—even an average team—doesn't draw the top high school players. They're recruited by everyone, so why pick a school that doesn't consistently win? In the pecking order of things, Dunster's job is on the line every game, which means our jobs are on the line too. When we don't win big—at least by a touchdown or two—Dunster has to answer to Brian, who gets flak from the Board of Regents. Every game we lose, alumni donations dwindle. It's all about the money." Chad helped himself to pretzels on the bar counter while waiting for his beer. "Remember Jerry McGuire?"

"Yeah," Eve replied, nibbling on a pretzel as well, "but if memory serves, Jerry bonded with his client in the end, so it was more than just showing him the money."

Chad laughed. "College football—or at least college administration—hasn't evolved that far. The bottom line is we're only looking for the best high school athletes to recruit, and to do that, we need to be on top."

Eve shook her head. "No wonder Brian's son doesn't want to play football."

"He mentioned his kid landed in your class. How's that going?"

"So far, so good. Trey was absent today, so I sent a text to Brenda."

"You planning to get cozy with the wife?"

"Hardly," Eve replied. "I'd rather not have any contact at all. It would keep things easier, but she requested the teachers inform her whenever Trey is absent. I'd rather not have her appearing in my doorway."

"Good idea. You don't want her catching on. The woman is smart."

Eve tried to keep the irritability out of her voice. "And I'm not?"

"All I'm saying is she likes being in control and won't take kindly to having her perfect little world turned upside down."

"I told you before I have no intention of upsetting any apple carts. Having a simple affair meets my needs—and Brian's—perfectly. I'm not looking to take anyone's husband away. I just want to borrow one for some fun."

Chad laughed again. "Too bad we've been friends for so long or I'd have taken you up on that after the divorce."

"Yeah, well, I sure don't want another miserable marriage." Eve picked up the second martini the bartender had automatically brought and changed the subject. "So how's your on-line affair going?"

"So-so. She's not quite as experienced as I like, but then, I plan to teach her a few things."

"Where did you say she worked?"

"I didn't."

Eve arched a brow. "You keeping it a secret?"

"Not exactly." Chad shrugged. "I think she said she was a secretary someplace. I wasn't really paying attention to the details."

"Sometimes paying attention to details can be very beneficial."

"Well, I pay attention to *some* details—like how big her boobs are or if she has enough padding to cushion the push-in. Nothing worse than riding a bony skeleton."

Eve shook her head. "You're incorrigible."

Chad grinned. "I know." His eyes cased the room, and he winked at a blonde who smiled back. "I think I'll check that out."

"Totally incorrigible," Eve repeated as he tossed some money onto the counter and made his way over to the blonde's table. "And one more reason I won't marry again."

Even though Chad had been the one who'd offered her the proverbial shoulder to cry on after she discovered her ex had spent her savings—a secret she had not shared with anyone—she probably would not have liked him if she hadn't known him since high school. His good looks and athletic ability had made him instantly popular when he'd arrived in the ninth grade. Only she knew his father had never been part of the picture and his grandmother had taken him in after his mother had been arrested for prostitution—a fact she'd discovered after he'd gotten into a bloody fight with another boy over a bottle of illegal whiskey and she'd offered Chad a ride to his grandmother's. She'd driven him around until he'd sobered up enough to go home, and during that time, he'd told her about his mother.

They'd never mentioned it again.

****

Chad suppressed a smile as he watched Molly carefully sipping her wine and spritzer at the Pendulum on Wednesday afternoon. She'd been nursing the weak drink for nearly an hour.

"Why don't you let me refresh that for you?"

"No, it's all right. I don't want to get tipsy again."

He did smile then. "I really don't think anyone can get tipsy on what you're drinking, especially at that rate. You're sure you wouldn't like a cold replacement?"

"Yes. I mean, no." Molly's cheeks turned pink. "No, I don't need a replacement."

Chad found the response intriguing. He couldn't remember when a woman had blushed in his presence, even when she was completely naked. Hell, most of the women he hit on could make a man blush at their boldness. Not that he was one to complain. He liked experimental, uninhibited females.

He had to admit, if he'd seen Molly in a bar instead of on Blog-Face, he probably would have passed her over. Her dishwater-blonde-brownish hair was nondescript and her expression more wholesome than come-hither. She reminded him more of Eliza Doolittle or one of the von Trapp kids—from those movies Angie insisted on watching over and over—than a twenty-first-century swinging single. Hell, if he mentioned swinging, Molly would probably think playground. And not the kind of playground he would have in mind either.

Still, she had mentioned on Blog-Face that she'd moved to Big D for adventure.

He'd dropped subtle innuendos about sexual intimacy, and each time Molly had quickly responded with assurances that she believed in giving and taking and how much she liked touching. Chad had meant oral sex, but he was beginning to think she hadn't gotten that message. More and more, he was convinced Molly might be the elusive virgin he'd never had—and the idea of seducing her was what truly intrigued him.

Molly was tapping her fingers to the beat of the Stones' "Time Is on My Side" and Chad wondered if it were an omen. "Would you like to dance?" he asked and gestured toward the tiny dance area in a corner of the bar.

She blushed again and then nodded, part of her hair falling forward over her face. "I'd like that very much."

As Chad took her hand and led her to the dance floor, he had a surreal moment, remembering how awkward and shy the girls had been at his own middle-school dances. Sweet Jesus, he hadn't thought about himself as a kid in years. He'd been none too confident either at thirteen, but that had changed when the girl across the street had come home from college and decided to practice her kissing skills. When he'd proved a quick and adept learner, she'd taught him a lot more—a whole lot more. After that, girls his own age held no appeal.

Well, this wasn't Kansas and he wasn't in middle school anymore.

Expertly, he slipped his arm around Molly's waist, bringing her close, but not too much. Part of the seduction process was building anticipation. Being near enough to feel body heat but not be assailed by it was a subtle tease. The fact that Molly rested her hand lightly on his shoulder rather than twining her arm around his neck told him he'd made the right move—which brought to mind Bob Seger's lyrics from "Night Moves"—but it was probably too early for that.

Since there were plenty of available women to satiate him, Chad would wait and let the desire build in him as well.

****

—Looking forward to next week, luv.—

—Me too. I am so glad I found you on Blog-Face! I never would have believed I could be so lucky.—

—I'm the lucky one, luv.—

Molly sighed contentedly, tapped the Close button, and stuck her cell in her desk, just as Mrs. Wilson sailed full-force through the lobby, frown on face.

"You look like a cat who's not only gotten into the cream but knows how to open the refrigerator door," Joni said as the principal passed by, leaving everyone looking busy in her wake.

"I know it's too early to tell, but I think I may have met 'the one.' "

"The on-line guy? How many times have you seen him?"

"Only two, but he's just so *nice*."

Joni smiled. "From his picture, I'd say he doesn't have to be *nice*. He's drop-dead gorgeous."

"Oh, yes! He's definitely cute. And romantic." Molly giggled. "He always calls me 'luv' because he knows how much I like British Retro."

Joni glanced around and lowered her voice. "So has he made a move yet?"

Molly felt her face heat. "No! He's a gentleman."

Joni snorted. "There's no such thing. They don't exist anymore."

"What doesn't exist anymore?" Mr. Conrad asked as he approached the desk, a sheaf of papers in his hand.

Molly's cheeks grew warmer at the embarrassing interruption, but Joni seemed unperturbed. "Gentlemen. Molly thinks she's found a knight-in-shining-armor."

Her face couldn't possibly get any hotter. Molly was afraid her head might explode into a fiery ball any moment. "She exaggerates, Mr. Conrad."

"Please call me Arthur," he replied and gave her a quizzical look. "If I may ask, where did you find this charming lad?"

"Blog-Face," Joni said before Molly could reply. "I gotta admit, the guy is hot."

Mr. Conrad raised a brow, and Molly prayed for an earthquake, or at least a tremor that would put a crack in the floor through which she could sink. How humiliating! She didn't even use words like "hot" let alone in front of another man. What in the world would Mr. Conrad—Arthur—think? "I never said that!"

Joni snickered. "You don't have to. Just looking at the guy's picture is enough. Definitely *hot*."

"Given that degree of heat, he'd probably melt the chain mail," Arthur said dryly.

Molly smiled in spite of her embarrassment. She'd always thought puns were funny. She liked the way Arthur's eyes twinkled too, even though he kept a straight face. "I haven't seen any piles of melded steel lying around."

Arthur smiled, revealing a dimple in one cheek. "The *gentleman* is probably alive and well, then." He laid his bundle of papers on the counter. "These are flyers for students who might be interested in the debate club. We could also use kids who know how to maintain the interactive website we're required to use for competition."

"I'll try to encourage them," Molly said, thankful the subject had been changed and equally glad the bell rang before Joni could get back on her track.

"You're not mad, are you?" Joni asked after Mr. Conrad left. "I was just teasing."

Molly shook her head. "I'm not angry. I know it's silly to get my hopes up."

"Ah, honey, it's not. Heck, I haven't had a date in six months. Your guy is…definitely *cute*, so I was living vicariously, that's all. It sounds like you had a really good time. When are you going to see him again?"

"Next Wednesday afternoon at the Pendulum," Molly replied.

"He *is* taking things slow then," Joni said. "With most guys, it's meet for a drink once, then make it an evening. Preferably on the weekend when getting to work the next morning isn't important, if you get what I mean."

Molly's face warmed again. "I don't think Chad would expect anything like that! Besides, he lives in Waco, so he only gets up to Dallas during the week on business."

Joni gave her a shrewd look. "The guy's not married, is he?"

"No, of course not."

"You sure?"

"Yes. He told me he was divorced." Molly frowned. "Why do you think he'd be married? I met him on Blog-

Face Singles Spot."

"Honey, sometimes people lie." Joni paused. "I just think it a bit odd that you've been on-line with him for several weeks, you've met twice in the middle of the week in the afternoon, and he hasn't mentioned doing anything on a weekend."

"That's easy to explain. He's a college football recruiter. He has to scout games all over Texas on weekends."

"Okay." Joni patted her hand. "Just be careful."

"There's nothing to worry about. Chad really is a gentleman. Maybe not a knight, but a gentleman."

"I sure hope so." Joni smiled and lightened the conversation. "Maybe you could clone him for me?"

Molly laughed too and undid the tie to the stack of papers Mr. Conrad had left. She knew there were men who cheated on their wives. There had even been a scandal or two in her hometown, but the men involved had been in their forties and fifties, going through what her mother called a male mid-life crisis.

Chad was too young for that. He had seemed genuinely sad when he'd told her how his wife had left him because he was gone so much and she wanted to be closer to her parents. He'd even choked up when he mentioned missing his small daughter. He was a man capable of deep feelings, so of course he wouldn't rush into anything.

Besides, he was a gentleman. Molly just knew it.

Chapter Seven

"Spaghetti again?" Chad asked the next evening as Angie opened a jar of sauce, poured it into a bowl, and stuck it in the microwave.

"It's quick and easy," she answered as she drained the pasta and ladled it onto two plates and then spooned sauce over the top. She held up a can of grated parmesan. "Want cheese?"

"Sure. Why not?"

Ignoring the sarcasm in his tone, Angie set the plates down and then went back to the microwave to heat a bowl of mac-and-cheese for Jessica, who was already banging her spoon on the top of her high chair.

Chad slammed his fork down. "Does she have to make so much racket?"

Startled at the sound, Jessica stared at him and then started crying.

"Damn it!"

Jessica cried louder.

"You're scaring her," Angie said as she hurried back to the table, half-warm bowl in hand. "There, there, sweetie," she said, spooning some of the gooey noodles into Jessica's mouth. "Daddy didn't mean it."

Chad sighed and picked up his fork. "I've had a rough day. Practice didn't go well, and if we lose on Saturday, Dunster is going to take it out on our hides."

"Maybe you should think about changing careers."

Fork half way to his mouth, Chad stared at her as though she'd taken leave of her senses. Which he probably thought she had.

"I'm just saying."

"Why the hell would I want to change careers? I love football."

Angie wiped dribble from Jessica's chin and wondered how much she should say. "You're just not home very much. I feel like I'm raising our daughter on my own."

Chad laid his fork on his plate. "We've discussed this before. I told you when you said you wanted to have kids that I wouldn't be around much. Coaching takes up a lot of time."

"I know that. I sat in the bleachers every Friday night when you were at the high school. I understand Saturdays are game days in college and Sundays you do replays, but you're gone Friday nights—"

"Because I have to scout the high school games. This season isn't going that well. Metro needs stronger, tougher players."

"What about the other nights? The past two Wednesdays—"

"Work, Angie. Work. I am working. There's more to coaching that just getting on the field. We study our opponents' plays, then the whole staff has to strategize. Each team is different. We have to plan both defensive and offensive moves based on that. I can't just drop everything at five o'clock to come home."

"It would be nice to have dinner together on a regular basis."

Chad looked down at his spaghetti, and Angie bit her lip. She knew what he was going to say. She held up her hand. "If I knew when you were coming home, I could cook something else."

He looked up. "Like what?"

"Well, like..." She hesitated, thinking about what she did know how to cook. "Maybe a tuna casserole or something."

"I hate tuna." Chad twirled strands of cold spaghetti on his fork and stuffed it into his mouth. "Never mind."

"I could fix something else, then. I just would like for you to spend more time at home with us."

Chad glanced at Jessica, who had stuck her fingers in the bowl and was smearing the mess on her bib. Angie quickly reached for a napkin to wipe the tiny hand. "Don't you want to be with your daughter?"

"Sweet Jesus." Chad picked up his plate, took it to the sink, and scraped the contents into the disposal. "You know I'm not good with little kids. I told you that before you got pregnant. You said it didn't matter."

Jessica began to cry again, and Angie removed her from the highchair to rock her, getting cheese goo on her shirt as well. "You didn't say you didn't want *anything* to do with kids. I thought once we had a baby, you'd change your mind."

A muscle twitched in Chad's jaw. "Look. I may not be a hands-on dad, but I'm at least providing for her. And for you too. Do you think it was easy on the budget when you left your full-time job for part-time? No, it wasn't, but I knew it was important for a child to have at least one parent at home most of the time. Coaching pays better than a lot of jobs. And those extra trips I take? I pad my expenses for a little extra cash."

"That's not honest!"

The muscle twitched again. "Everyone does it. Brian

just signs off on the accounts. I doubt he even looks at them."

"But still—"

"Don't worry about it." Chad turned toward the hall. "I'm going to be working on the computer for a while. Don't wait up."

After he'd gone, Angie left the dirty dishes on the table and carried a still-fussy Jessica into the living room. Settling into her favorite rocker, Angie began to croon softly, to calm both her daughter and herself.

She'd been so sure Chad would change his mind once the baby arrived. Who wouldn't love a baby? Angie fingered Jessica's soft curls and ran a finger down the silky-smooth cheek. She could maybe understand that Chad would feel awkward with a small child, especially a girl, but shouldn't that be all the more reason to spend time with her? Maybe she needed to point out that girls could be athletes too. When Jessica got a bit older, Chad could teach her to play softball and soccer and whatever else. Angie smiled to herself. Surely, he would like that idea.

Meanwhile, maybe she could convince Chad to be here for dinner if she learned to cook. What man wouldn't want to come home if he knew a real meal waited for him?

Tomorrow, she would call Brenda Caldwell and ask where to go for cooking classes. Every dinner or party she'd ever attended at the Caldwells' had always had delicious food. Brenda would steer her in the right direction.

"It's a start," Angie whispered to her daughter. "I'll bring your daddy home. Just wait and see."

****

Chad closed the door to the office, tempted to lock it. But that would bring more accusations should Angie try to open it. He could always link quickly to the Metro website if she happened to come in.

He sat down and opened his Blog-Face account, thankful it was not only protected with passwords but its actual existence could also be hidden, which was probably why it had surpassed its competitors in users. Chad ran a hand through his hair, thinking about what he wanted to say to Molly. He sure as hell didn't want to sound needy, although what he *needed* was a good lay. Not that he could confront a possible virgin with that kind of bluntness.

When had Angie lost her attractiveness for him anyhow? When he'd met her six years ago, she had been cute, curvy, and vivacious. Ready to party and more than willing to follow his lead in sexual experimentation. Even when they'd married, a year later, the honeymoon had been smokin' hot, in spite of the fact that they'd rented a cabin in New England in December. Angie had said she wanted a white Christmas, since she'd never seen one. She didn't see much of that one either, since they spent more of their time in bed than out of it.

Gradually, though, that had changed when they returned to Texas. His wife was still eager to have sex, but it was because she wanted to start a family right away. He'd suggested they give themselves some time. Angie had reluctantly agreed, but Chad began to suspect she wasn't taking the pill. He hated wearing condoms, so he'd done Internet research about timing and began restricting himself to those days of the month that would be safe.

Angie hadn't liked that and began having headaches

at bedtime.

Which was when other women started looking *really* attractive.

Chad sighed and turned back to Blog-Face, typing in Eve's name. She would understand his predicament. Maybe. Or, at least, she wouldn't judge him. She never had, which was probably why he actually respected her.

—Been a bummer tonight.—

—Argument?—

—Big time. Wants me home at nights.—

—Hmmm. Not a possibility?—

—Hate being cooped up. Need to get out.—

—Do you want to meet at our watering hole?—

—Wish I could. Restricted tonight.—

—That bad, huh?—

—Just better not to pick another argument.—

—Indulge in fantasy then.—

—With you?—

—Funny. Ha. Ha.—

—Just thought I'd try, sweetness. Manana.—

—In your dreams. Manana.—

Chad grinned to himself, in spite of the rejection. Eve and he had long ago clarified their boundaries, but sometimes they both enjoyed bantering back and forth. Truth be told, he kind of liked having her put him in his place now and then. He'd often wondered if Eve had a little dominatrix in her. Speaking of which, indulging in fantasy wasn't a bad idea. He sure couldn't Blog-Face Molly when he was this horny—he'd say something wrong.

All was silent in the house, so maybe Angie had taken Jessica upstairs. Chad clicked on his favorite porn site, making sure he had the Metro U link up just in case the door opened. Fifteen minutes later—he'd need to dispose of some tissues before he went to bed—he felt somewhat better. Switching back to Blog-Face, he entered Molly's name.

—Hey, luv. What do you say to dinner next Wednesday?—

—I'd "luv" that!—

—Fantastic. Dress up. We'll do fancy.—

—Super!—

—See you then. I'll dream of you, luv.—

—Oooh! How romantic!—

Chad logged off the site with a satisfied sigh. Nothing like a fancy dinner to bring out the romance in a girl. He could pad his expense account to cover it.

And maybe he just might make a little night move.

****

"Thanks for letting me come over," Angie said Saturday afternoon as she settled Jessica on Brenda's sofa. "I know you have a busy schedule this close to Thanksgiving."

"Most of the charities are fundraising like crazy right now," Brenda agreed. "I had a meeting this morning with one of them and another scheduled for later this afternoon, but I've got an hour free. What's on your mind? You sounded a little anxious when you called."

"I want to learn to cook."

Brenda blinked at her. "Cook?"

"Yes. I—" Angie suddenly noticed an applesauce stain on her sweater sleeve. It must have happened cleaning up Jessica's breakfast this morning. She rolled the cuff into her palm, hoping Brenda wouldn't notice. "I want to start preparing better meals for Chad and me."

"Has Chad developed an urge to start eating healthy or something?"

"No." This was so embarrassing. "I just thought...well, maybe if he had home-cooked meals, he'd look forward to them."

Brenda smiled. "Are you thinking about that old adage that the way to a man's heart is through his stomach?"

"No...yes..." Angie hoped she wasn't blushing. She hated when she did that. "Well, maybe."

Brenda's smile broke into a gentle laugh. "I think that concept went out of favor when men discovered buffalo wings."

Angie looked at her, confused. "But your meals are always delicious. Full courses, the table set with china and silver. Even flowers. Your family must appreciate all of that."

Brenda shook her head. "I do that for me because I like a pleasant environment. I doubt my son even notices, intent as he is on stuffing food into his mouth so he can be excused to get back on that ridiculous Blog-Face. Brian is seldom home..." She paused and studied Angie. "It that what this is about? Chad not coming home for dinner?"

Angie felt her face heat. She was probably as red as a sunset. She pulled more of her cuff into her palm. "He is gone a lot."

"Coaches do keep long hours."

"I know. It was bad enough when Chad coached high school and had to teach during the day and coach after school. The Friday night games were kinda fun, and I put up with the weekend post-game meetings. I just thought when he moved up to college level, the hours would get better."

"Unfortunately, they don't," Brenda replied, "and the pressure to win is much worse—and more political."

"I know that too. Chad's told me often enough. It's just…just… Well, Jessica's growing up, and she hardly knows her father."

Brenda glanced at Jessica, who had fallen asleep leaning against Angie. Her face softened. "I felt the same way when my boys were small."

"So what did you do?"

"When they were toddlers, there wasn't much I could do. When Tom, the older one, got involved in Little League, Brian started bonding with him. Trey has never been interested in sports." Brenda shrugged. "You just have to be the best mother you can."

"I love Jessica more than anything in life. I love being a mother. I just want Chad to be there for her too."

Brenda leaned over and patted Angie's hand. "You can't force him, dear."

"I know." Angie looked down at her sleeping daughter and then at Brenda. "But I still think if I had nice, hot meals ready, he'd be home more. I want to learn to cook."

Brenda laughed softly and sat back. "So be it, then. Every battle has its strategy. We'll see if yours works."

****

Brenda's committee meeting ran later than she'd anticipated, and it was nearly six-thirty before she headed home. She was all too aware of the irony of her conversation earlier this afternoon as she stopped at her favorite Italian deli to pick up a calzone.

Equally ironic—but not surprising—the house was empty when she got there. So much for cooking, homemade or otherwise. Popping the calzone in the oven, Brenda poured a Merlot, went into the parlor, and turned on a Mozart CD, the soft strains soothing after a long day of meetings. She settled herself on the sofa where Angie had sat this afternoon and reflected.

She could well sympathize with Angie. The girl was barely past her twenties and still caught up in the romantic idea of love and marriage. Sometimes, Brenda could hardly believe she'd been that young or naïve herself. The summer in Newport, when she'd met Brian, seemed like an eternity ago, not just twenty-five years.

He'd shown up on the beach, all rippling muscle, skin bronzed, his inky hair nearly blue in the sunlight. Every female on the beach had fastened shaded eyes on him. Probably half of them would have swooned—if they hadn't already been lying on the sand—when he gave them his slow grin, and spoke with his Texas twang. Brenda had considered herself lucky when she was the one who'd "caught" him.

Silly girl.

Brian had been all too aware of his attractiveness. She'd spent the first few years they were together fending off rivals, doing everything she could to please Brian. Buying sexy lingerie, never refusing him in bed, making sure she was the perfect "coach's wife" by never complaining, and keeping his favorite meals warm until he came home.

Cooking.

Brenda sipped her wine and closed her eyes. She hadn't had the heart to tell Angie none of it would work.

Brian had his first affair—or at least, the first one she found out about—right after Tom was born. And, like Angie, Brenda had thrown herself into motherhood, delighted to start a family. And, like Angie, she had been flummoxed to realize Brian didn't share her joy.

And, like Brian, if Brenda's suspicions were correct, Chad was having an affair.

Everything she'd told Angie this afternoon was basically true. Coaches did work long hours and there was a special camaraderie among the ranks, not to mention their macho love of football. Still, over the years, she'd met plenty of them who loved being family men and who clearly cared about their wives.

Whether they cooked or not. Brenda smiled, remembering a good friend years ago who'd hardly been able to open a can of beans without cutting herself and whose idea of dinner meant deciding which Styrofoam box of take-out to remove from the fridge. Her husband had practically worshiped the ground she walked on. Vaguely, she wondered what had happened to them. Maybe she should actually get on Blog-Face herself and look them up.

Her text dinged, bringing her out of reverie. Trey had actually sent her a message, saying he was at a meeting the Tech Club was having at Starbucks.

Brenda sent a response and set the phone down. She'd have to check out the Tech Club on Monday, make sure it was legit. The last thing she needed was for Trey to be lying. Brian would send her son off to that horrid boot camp with no hesitation.

While Brenda couldn't assure Angie her husband would not cheat, one thing she did tell her was true—to be the best mother one could be.

That was all they could really do.

Chapter Eight

"Christ, you're hot, and so wet."

"Mmmm." Eve tucked her hands behind her head so she wouldn't be tempted to reach for Brian as he spread her legs even wider, sliding fingers inside her as his mouth sucked on a beaded nipple. "Mmmm," she said again and arched her back to give him better access to her breasts. Already, her body was tensing, her vagina clenching in a series of small spasms attempting to hold tight to the forceful motion of his fingers, plundering her.

"Come for me, babe."

"I—oh, my God!" Eve gasped and tried to prolong the moment, even as her body convulsed, every nerve ending on fire. "Ahhh!"

"Very good, babe. Finish me?"

Eve nodded. In a deft movement, Brian slid himself into her passage and she wrapped her legs tightly around him while he thrust deeply, spending himself.

When they could both finally speak, Eve rolled on her side. "I really didn't expect to see you tonight, since it's Saturday."

"We had a good game. Big win. I wanted to celebrate."

She ran her hand slowly across his chest, her fingers lightly grazing his flat nipple. "Want to keep celebrating?"

He took her hand and lowered it to his shaft. "Let's

see if the Big Guy is up to it."

Eve laughed and began to stroke his already hardening length. "I believe he is."

****

First period on Monday mornings was never pleasant. Most of the kids were tardy and they came in either grumpy or overly excited, depending on what kind of a weekend they'd had.

Eve grimaced, realizing she was no different from her straggling students. She'd had fantastic sex Saturday, not that she could talk about it to anyone. Being truly free of emotional commitment, but exquisitely attuned to the sexual wants and needs of a partner was heady stuff, much better than any drug the kids could drop. But, like a drug wearing off, the sensational sizzling fizzled in the gloomy light of a dreary, rainy day. The note Molly left in her box noting Brenda Caldwell wanted to see her only added to the grim reality of Monday.

Eve glanced to where Trey sat slouched in his seat near the back of the room. His long black hair covered half his face and, as usual, his dark eyes watched her. For a moment she had the uncomfortable feeling she was prey on which he waited to pounce. She shook the feeling off. He had been nothing but polite. She was just unsettled because of having to deal with his mother. Eve really didn't like complications.

To her surprise, one of the girls from Arthur Conrad's debate team sat down next to Trey and gave him a smile. To Eve's even greater surprise, Trey smiled back, actually looking interested. She hid her own grin. Ravati Singh was as unlikely a flirt as the plant on Eve's desk. Both of her parents were professors at Metro U, and most likely she would be valedictorian of her class

75

next year when she was a senior. Arthur had told the faculty the girl should definitely be a lawyer, since she had the ability to ferret out the tiniest bit of misinformation and use it against her opponent in tournaments. The IT teacher had argued Ravati should go to MIT and then on to take over Apple someday. In any event, the girl was seriously studious, wielding a paintbrush as carefully as she would a scalpel. Even though Eve made it a point not to have favorites, Ravati actually seemed interested in art. If she had chosen to befriend Trey, so much the better.

Which is what Eve told Brenda when they met on her conference period.

"I'm glad to hear he's made a friend of good standing," Brenda replied. "As you know, I've been concerned he might attach himself to the wrong group of students. Do you know if she's a member of the Technology Club?"

"Probably." Eve smiled, glad the conversation was staying on a positive note. "I doubt Mr. Thatcher, her IT teacher, would have let her get away."

"So the club did meet on Saturday afternoon?"

"I'm not sure, but that sounds right. Mr. Thatcher likes to give his students plenty of time to work on creating new programs." Brenda looked relieved, and Eve felt a bit of sympathy for her. It couldn't be easy having a kid who'd not only gotten kicked out of a class but also arrested. "That group should be pretty safe."

"Well, that's good then," Brenda said. "I knew my husband was celebrating the big win Saturday with the coaches, but I wasn't sure about Trey."

Eve focused on gathering her notebook and pen. Brian had celebrated all right—just not with the coaches, unless she counted the guiding of his hands to all the right spots, *coaching*. She rose. "Excuse me, but I've got to get back to class."

"Of course," Brenda replied, standing as well. "I'm glad to know I can count on your help."

Eve gave Brenda a brief nod, wanting nothing more than to get away. Things were getting complicated.

****

The next day, Trey handed Eve an envelope before he went to his seat. She eyed it speculatively. "What's this?"

He shrugged. "Don't know. Mom told me to give one to each of my teachers."

Eve breathed a small sigh of relief. At least it wasn't a personal note, then. Tempted as she was to open it, there were thirty pairs—all the students were present for once—of curious eyes watching her. Not wanting to embarrass Trey, Eve slipped the paper inside her purse. "Thank you."

She didn't have time to read it at lunch, either, since some enterprising student had pulled a fire alarm earlier, which not only brought out the fire department but several of the superintendent's minions as well. Mrs. Wilson's regular scowl had deepened while dealing with them, and she had emailed the faculty to meet with her during their afternoon planning periods. Determined as a terrier at a rabbit hole, she wanted a list of every student who'd been out of the classroom with a pass at the time the alarm was triggered.

Eve had been tempted to point out that whoever had done it was probably roaming the halls *without* a pass, but she didn't think the principal was interested in logic at the moment. When Central Office staff showed up, they always wanted things in writing, CYA in case Board members inquired.

So it wasn't until Eve was in her apartment later, wrapped in her favorite robe, that she retrieved the envelope. Inside was a handwritten note on personalized stationery—who even used stationery anymore?—inviting Eve to a Saturday lunch at the Hilton Anatole in two weeks as a thank-you for being so much help with Trey.

Of course, she wouldn't go. The school district frowned on anything that might be considered a bribe, even though Eve suspected that in Brenda Caldwell's charitable world, this was simply the way things were done. But Eve had always been careful not to accept gifts, not to mention spending personal time with Brian's wife was a complication she did not need.

Knowing Brian had a wife was one thing, although at this point, Eve would have preferred never even to have met Brenda. Since Joe's theft of her savings—and her trust—Eve had taken great care that nothing and no one would wreak havoc with her life again. Everything fit into neat little compartments. When she was at school, she was professional and didn't play favorites with her students. Her personal life was structured. She socialized superficially with her colleagues, had several *real* friends from college days she stayed in touch with, and kept her sexual life private. Everything was neat and orderly, just the way it should be.

Damn it. Eve needed to talk to Chad. She didn't agree with everything he did, but at least he'd understand her dilemma. She contemplated asking him to meet her at their bar, but she was really too tired to get dressed again and go out.

Taking her mini-tab from the end table, she logged on to Chad's Blog-Face.

—Got a minute?—

—Sure. WU?—

—Got an invite from Trey's mom.—

—Where to?—

—Lunch. Anatole. All Trey's teachers.—

—Cool.—

—Not really. Don't want to go.—

—Free food. Why not go?—

—You know why. She's Brian's wife, for God's sake.—

—One reason you should go.—

—Huh?—

—So she won't suspect anything.—

—She won't be able to suspect anything if I am not there.—

—If you're the only one missing, she might.—

—God, it's getting complicated.—

—One reason I don't hang around long. Play cougar, get a boy toy.—

—Not really interested in toys.—

—You might change your mind.—

—Doubtful. Better go.—

—See ya.—

Eve clicked off and tossed the tablet back on the table, shaking her head at Chad's suggestion. Boy toys. She definitely did not need to hover in bars, competing with twenty-somethings in six-inch stilettos, nor did she have the gift of blarney that Chad did. Irish she might be, but her inner Scorpio liked working behind the scenes instead of front stage center. Besides, she preferred the company of strong men who knew their own minds, not someone who just wanted to party. In that respect, she and Brian were a good match. If only his wife would stay in the neat little compartment Eve had assigned her to, things would be perfect.

****

"Of course, you will attend." Mrs. Wilson looked over the rim of her glasses at Eve. "Why in the world would you not want to?"

Damn it. Eve hadn't expected to have a meeting first thing Tuesday morning, but a note was in her box that all Trey's teachers were to meet with the principal before school. She'd thought Mrs. Wilson was going to warn them not to accept "gifts," but the principal had done just the opposite. Maybe because she'd gotten an invitation too. "I thought Central Administration frowned on this kind of thing."

"Normally they would, but this isn't just a luncheon." Mrs. Wilson picked up her envelope and removed a handful of tickets. "It is a very worthy fundraiser."

Eve stared at her. She had no idea the lunch had a purpose. Brenda hadn't mentioned that in her note. She caught a glimpse of one ticket as Mrs. Wilson waved them around. "Is that the Metroplex Happy Holidays Extravaganza?"

"It is! The largest—and most prestigious—holiday fundraiser of the year!"

"Somewhat like the Texas Cattlemen's Ball in Fort Worth," Mr. Conrad said.

Mrs. Wilson nodded. "Besides a silent auction, there will be celebrities performing at the luncheon. I think the governor even attended last year, since the fundraiser benefits so many different charities. The superintendent was quite pleased to learn we've been invited."

"I wonder how Mrs. Caldwell was able to get tickets for all of us?" Mr. Thatcher asked. "My wife has always wanted to go, but the tickets usually sell out right away."

"I think Mrs. Caldwell is chairperson for the event," Mr. Conrad replied. "Trey mentioned something about it."

"Well, it was very kind of her to include us," Mrs. Wilson said as the warning bell rang for first period. She frowned at Eve. "I expect each of you to be there."

Just spiffy. Eve gathered her things and hurried to her class. Brenda had been very clever in sending the tickets to the principal, knowing that administrators, like politicians, took every opportunity to promote the schools. Not that it was a bad thing to do, but having the principal receive the tickets ensured that none of the teachers would decline. Not only was Eve going to have to spend several hours making small talk with people she didn't know—and God help them if anyone running for office showed up!—but she was going to have to socialize with Brian's wife, too. It was bad enough to have to meet with her and deliver behavior reports, but Eve really didn't want to be beholden to Brenda for anything.

Why couldn't the woman just stay in her own world and out of Eve's?

Chapter Nine

Chad motioned to the bartender for another beer and a Scotch for Brian. "Good game last Saturday. You missed a great party afterward." Then he grinned. "I suspect you had a party anyhow."

Brian raised a brow and gave him a sideways glance. "What's that supposed to mean?"

"Ah, come on. I know you're doing Eve."

"Keep your voice down," Brian said as the bartender set their drinks on the counter. "I'd rather not have all of Dallas County know."

"Sorry." Chad glanced around. At five o'clock on a Wednesday afternoon, there was hardly anyone in the neighborhood bar. "I think your secret is safe."

"I want to keep it that way. Christ, if Brenda found out, there'd be hell to pay."

"Yeah, well, hope she doesn't. Eve mentioned your kid enrolled in her art class. Makes things kind of cozy, doesn't it?"

"Too cozy. I planned to send Trey to the camp in Parker County, but Brenda wanted to give him a chance at another school. She's way too soft on him."

Chad flashed back, momentarily, to his own high school days. With the hours his mother kept, she hadn't had time for him. After the arrest, his grandmother had taken him in, willing to start parenting again at age sixty. He could still remember going home in the afternoons to the aroma of fresh-baked bread or the alluring scent of homemade pie. Then his mother had gotten out of prison and taken him back. Resolutely, Chad pushed those thoughts away.

"Well, maybe giving the kid one more chance isn't a bad idea."

Brian swilled his Scotch. "Maybe. I just wish they hadn't chosen Deer Hill. I'd like to keep Eve as far away from Brenda as possible."

"Kinda hard to do, given the circumstances."

"I know. My wife hovers over Trey, which doesn't make it any easier."

"Eve's smart. She won't give anything away."

"I'm not worried about Eve talking. It's just that my wife has a way of prying into other people's lives and ferreting out useful information. That's one of the reasons she's so successful at fundraising—a little dirt on someone is good incentive for that person to donate— but I don't like her sticking her nose into Trey's teachers' business."

Chad frowned. "You know about the lunch, right?"

Brian set his glass down, giving Chad an appraising look. "What lunch?"

"I assumed Eve told you. She got an invitation yesterday. Brenda invited Trey's teachers to lunch at the Anatole."

"Why? Never mind," Brian answered his own question. "It's one of Brenda's maneuvers to manipulate. Damn it all."

"No need to worry. Eve said the district frowns on gifts, so she's not going."

"I wish Eve had told me."

Chad shrugged, ignoring the irritation in Brian's

voice. "Eve makes her own decisions. Since she decided not to go, she probably didn't think it was worth bugging you about it."

"Still, it's something I need to know. To protect myself—and Eve—from Brenda, if nothing else."

"Well, talk to Eve, then. I gotta go." Chad slid off the barstool and threw some bills on the counter. "Got a hot date with that chick I met on line."

"Another one?"

"Nah, the same one I've taken out for drinks twice. Think I'll make a move tonight, though."

Brian shook his head. "I can't keep up with your escapades. How do you juggle all your women?"

Chad laughed. "It's not so much juggling as it is serial dating."

"None of them come back to haunt you?"

"Nope. Show 'em a good time, have a little fun— the secret is not hanging around long enough for anyone to get too close."

"For you or them?"

Chad studied Brian for a moment. "Both," he finally said.

****

Chad pulled on a navy sports coat as he parked his car in front of Molly's apartment building. He'd contemplated actually wearing a tie, but decided the open collar of his chambray shirt had a better effect. Ties made men appear uptight, if not downright stuffy— neither an image he wanted. The khaki pants and topsiders gave him a casual look, perfect for the trendy bistro where he was taking Molly.

His mouth almost dropped, though, when she opened her door. From the floppy-brimmed hat pulled down over her hair to the frilly, high-necked blouse, loose jacket, and long skirt with boots, she looked like she'd stepped off the set for *Annie Hall*. Had Molly misunderstood when he'd told her the restaurant was casual-chic? That meant designer jeans, spiky heels, and something low cut, preferably with spaghetti straps that could be easily slipped down later. Instead, he was going to have to peel off layers of clothes, something he'd rarely ever had to do—although perhaps it would be fun. Kind of like strip poker. Yeah. One tantalizing piece of clothing at a time, like unwrapping a present. The thought made him smile.

Molly beamed back at him. "You're right on time!"

Women liked that. Score a point. "I didn't want to keep you waiting." For some absolutely unknown reason, he offered her his arm. "Shall we go?"

She locked her door and handed him the key. "Would you hold onto this?"

His mouth almost gaped again. Molly was handing him her key? Was that a clearly open invitation for later? Score another point. "I'd be delighted to."

"I didn't want to drag my purse along."

Her purse. Chad's brain was having trouble catching up with her words. What woman didn't carry a purse? If for no other reason than to have her cell phone handy. He couldn't remember the last time he'd sat across from a woman who didn't have it lying on the table. "No phone?" he asked and then could have bitten his own tongue for bringing it up.

"Oh, no. Mom never allowed them at dinner. Besides, it would be rude not to concentrate on my date."

He smiled as he helped her into the car. "I plan to concentrate on you too, luv."

His concentration would center on how to remove those clothes in a very sexy way, although perhaps it was best not to mention that just yet.

Molly giggled. "You are such a gentleman!"

Chad bit back a grin as he slipped behind the wheel. If she wanted a gentleman, he could act the part. Hell, he could play a damn knight in shining armor if it got her clothes off. More and more, he was finding her naïveté refreshing. Kind of like seducing Little Red Riding Hood. The big, bad wolf had every intention of eating her, too—or at least nibbling.

Molly looked around with awe in her eyes when they got to the Italian restaurant. The façade on the outside was weathered brick, the massive oak door lit by old-fashioned brass lamps hanging on either side. The walls of the foyer inside were rough-hewn wood, the floor cobblestoned. Walking through two rows of marble pillars, some partially "broken," gave the impression of entering the Colosseum. Beyond, more brass lamps gave a warm glow to the dining room, the small tables discreetly intimate behind artfully arranged plants and palms. Soft strains of violin and cello from a string quartet in the recess of a small alcove lent to the ambiance.

"It's wonderful!" Molly exclaimed. "I feel like I'm in Italy!"

"*Grazie, signorina,*" the waiter who seated them said. "We try very hard."

"It truly is beautiful," Molly said, still gazing around, her eyes wide.

The young man smiled, his dark eyes twinkling. "*Sei bella—*"

"We'd like a bottle of Chianti," Chad interrupted.

He was not about to let Molly become dazzled by a kid complimenting her in Italian.

To his credit—or maybe realizing his tip could be in jeopardy—the waiter dipped his head in Chad's direction. "*Certo, signore. Il classico?*"

"Fine."

"Ooh, I like the way he talks," Molly said as the waiter left to get their wine.

Chad hoped Molly wasn't going to go fan over the guy. "It's part of the atmosphere. Why don't you decide what you'd like to eat?"

Molly looked down at the menu. "How cute! The items have the Italian names written right after the English ones!"

"Good for us, then." Chad smiled. "We'll know what we're ordering."

"You're funny." Molly scanned the offerings. "Why don't you just choose something for both of us?"

Chad raised an eyebrow. Molly really was a throwback to some other time period. He could just imagine what Eve would say if he—or any man—decided to order for her. Or, for that matter, Angie—although she'd probably order spaghetti. Whatever. Time to play the charming gentleman again.

"How about the veal scallopini? And perhaps some stuffed tomatoes?"

"Sounds wonderful."

Chad tilted his head to look at her. "Are you always so easy to please?"

"Not in everything."

With any other woman, that phrase would have been coy and suggestive, but Molly was looking at him with a totally guileless expression. Could any grown woman be so naïve? Chad found the idea strangely intriguing.

What the heck. If he were going to play the gentleman, he might as well do the whole Prince Charming thing. Maybe it would pay off later. Chad motioned for one of the violinists to come over. "Something romantic for the lady."

"*Si, signore.*"

Given the look of delighted rapture on Molly's face, Chad figured the ten-dollar tip for the song was worth it. He'd just add it on to his expense account anyhow.

"Thank you so much!" Molly gushed after the man had returned to his quartet. "I've never had anyone do something like that for me before."

Bingo. Not a bad start at all. "Someone certainly should have." From the way she blushed, he realized she wasn't used to getting compliments either. Amazing. Chad glanced around to see if there was one of those flower girls who sold roses from a basket, but he didn't see any. Perhaps just as well.

By the time Chad parked the car later and walked Molly to her door, he was hopeful she'd invite him in. The dinner had gone well, and he'd managed to convince her a half-bottle of wine was fine with a full meal. Her cheeks were flushed and her eyes a bit hazed, but he'd taken care she didn't get drunk. Uninhibited women were fun. Drunk women were not.

Molly turned at the door and held out her hand. "Thank you for a wonderful evening. I really enjoyed it."

Chad took her hand in both of his. "Aren't you going to invite me in for a nightcap?"

She looked confused. "I've had enough to drink. Besides, it's a school night."

Chad didn't press the point. Instead, he tugged her

toward him. Placing two fingers beneath her chin, he lifted her face and bent down, brushing his lips across hers in a slow, leisurely way—a kiss meant to tease.

He felt Molly's body stiffen, and he lightly stroked her shoulder and upper arm, being careful not to graze a breast. He didn't want her bolting inside like a frightened rabbit. He brushed her lips again, still lightly, and felt her begin to relax. Encouraged, he slid his hand behind her head, angling it for a more thorough kiss. Her lips moved against his, although she didn't open for him. With a lingering sigh, he finished the kiss and stepped back. Molly's eyes were glazed, her pupils dilated, her breath shallow. She was aroused, although he doubted if she recognized the feeling.

He bit back a grin. Seducing a virgin was going to be very interesting.

****

—Had great time at dinner last night, luv. Especially "dessert" :-)—

Molly sighed contentedly and stored her cell phone in her purse under the counter. She just had to look at the message one more time before she began her day. Not only was Chad drop-dead gorgeous, he was also *nice*. Gallant, even. The dinner had been the most incredible night of her life. Everything had been perfect. Just perfect. She'd never been serenaded before. And Chad's kiss! OMG. Even now, her face grew hot as the heated memory of the kiss coursed through her body—and she'd spent a good two hours reliving it before she went to sleep. OMG. Molly had not known a man's lips could be so firm and yet so tender. Or so warm and pliant. Or—

"From the look on your face, dinner must have been something else," Joni said as she handed Molly a stack of papers, "but you better look busy because Mrs. Wilson is on the way."

Quickly, Molly started to shuffle papers. She didn't want another reprimand, and the principal looked like she was loaded for bear, as Molly's daddy used to say. She stifled a giggle at the image and then sobered at the thought of Mrs. Wilson brandishing a gun instead of a radio.

The woman paused in front of the desk. "Are those the notices that need to go into the teachers' boxes?"

Molly had no idea, since she hadn't even looked at them. She did now. "Yes. They're the flyers about Fall Festival next week."

"Well, they should be in the boxes before 8:45 a.m. Teachers are supposed to pick up their mail before school starts."

"Yes, ma'am." Lord, she didn't seem to be able to do anything right when it came to the principal. She rose. "I'll put them right in."

Mrs. Wilson nodded and marched off. Molly heard a soft chuckle behind her.

"Don't let her get to you," Eve said as she tossed most of what had been in her box in the trash. "Fall Festival has been on the calendar for weeks." She looked over to Arthur Conrad and John Thatcher, both of whom were sorting their mail as well. "Either of you not heard about Fall Festival next week?"

John snickered. "Yeah, the social event of the season for Deer Hill."

Molly widened her eyes. "Is it a holiday performance of something?"

"Hardly." Arthur smiled and held out his hand. "Let me help you with those."

Molly hesitated. "I don't want Mrs. Wilson thinking I'm not doing my job."

"Don't worry. She's on Tardy Patrol right now," John said.

"Give me." Arthur took half the stack and started stuffing them into the pigeonholes. "Administration always gets stressed this time of year."

"But the holidays should be fun!"

"For some people they are," Arthur said neutrally.

Eve glanced at him. "But not for everyone."

"True." He took a deep breath and shoved the last of the papers into a hole. "There. I'd better get going before I'm tardy too."

After the teachers left, Molly looked at Joni. "What did Ms. O'Connor mean? Did something happen to her that she doesn't like Thanksgiving or Christmas?"

"She got divorced last year, although I don't think that had anything to do with it. What she was probably referring to was Mr. Conrad losing his wife just before Christmas last year."

"I'm so sorry! I didn't know. What happened?"

"Car accident. A norther blew through, and the rain turned to sleet. Trista—his wife—was returning from shopping. A truck skidded into her lane and totaled the car."

"Dear Lord. How awful."

Joni nodded. "Mr. Conrad took it pretty hard. They'd only been married a year or so."

"The poor man."

"He doesn't like to talk about it, so don't let him know I told you."

"But talking about it might be helpful. Healing, even."

"It's not that. He went through grief counseling. He's just a private person and doesn't want anyone feeling sorry for him." Joni reached for the ringing phone as Mrs. Wilson swept through on her way back to her office. "He's the stoic type."

Molly returned to her desk. She couldn't imagine the pain Arthur Conrad had gone through. To lose someone you loved—and he always seemed so pleasant and nice.

Nice, but nice in a different way from Chad. Molly reached for her cell once more to look again at the message. If Chad kept treating her like he did last night, "luv" might just become "love."

And, if this relationship blossomed, how could she bear to lose him? That would be the worst fate ever.

****

Thursday night. This morning, Chad had promised he would be home early. Angie suspected he'd agreed so easily because he had been so late last night. He'd said he'd had drinks with Brian and one thing led to another and he'd caught a bite before he came home. She'd been tempted to call Brenda and ask if Brian had been late too, but then decided it would be just too humiliating to ask.

Angie looked at the kitchen table, which also served as their dining room table, and moved the forks to the left side of the plates. It had been so long since she'd actually set a table, she'd nearly forgotten where the silverware went. Not that the flatware was real silver. The plates weren't china, either, and some were chipped around the edges, but they would have to do.

She peeked into the oven at the casserole. Chad didn't like tuna, but she hoped he'd like the chicken, rice, and broccoli one she had made. Since she'd never excelled at cooking, it seemed the simplest recipe she could find. And she'd been delighted to find prepared cookie dough at the grocery store. All she needed to do was slice and bake.

Maybe preparing meals wouldn't be so hard after all.

Jessica beat on the highchair tray with a spoon, reminding Angie her daughter was waiting. Quickly, she took the toddler's ready-to-go meal out of the microwave and helped Jessica eat. She hadn't bothered trying to find a sitter—this was supposed to be a family night, not a date, something Angie hoped Chad would find himself liking and be willing to come home to often.

Hearing his car in the driveway, Angie took the casserole out of the oven to cool and placed the sheet of cookies in. Brushing crumbs off her shirt, she hoped she hadn't splattered anything on it she didn't see.

Chad appeared in the doorway and glanced around. "Are you cooking?"

Angie beamed at him. "I thought I'd surprise you."

He looked at the set table. "This is different. We usually eat in front of the TV."

"Not tonight. I was talking to Brenda the other day and realized everything is always perfect at her house. Not that this is perfect," Angie said hastily as Jessica threw her spoon on the floor, "but I thought you might like to sit at the table for a change."

"Well, sure," Chad said, starting toward a chair just as Jessica picked up her bowl and prepared to launch it as well. He grabbed it before it flew through the air, but couldn't stop the mushy remainder of whatever had been inside from spilling over his hand. Biting back choice words, he placed the bowl on the counter and wiped his hand with a towel. "How old do they have to be before they can be taught table manners?"

"Soon," Angie replied. "I'll give her some crackers to keep her occupied. Go ahead and sit."

He did, eyeing Jessica warily. "She doesn't have any more weaponry, does she?"

Angie giggled as she spooned casserole onto plates and set them down. "No, but she's developing a pretty good throwing arm, don't you think?"

"Ummm. When she gets old enough, I'll see what she can do with a softball."

"Oh, that would be wonderful!"

Chad furrowed his brows and looked at her quizzically. "When did you take an interest in athletics?"

"Not me," Angie replied. "It would be a great way for you to bond with your daughter. Lots of fathers coach little girls' teams."

His eyes widened, almost as if in shock. "We'll see," he said in a noncommittal tone and dug into the casserole.

Angie watched him chew, suddenly remembering she hadn't heated up the dinner rolls. "Damn."

"What?"

"I forgot the bread."

"Never mind. Bread isn't that good for you anyhow."

"How's the casserole? Do you like it?"

He took another bite. "Not bad." Then he raised his head and sniffed. "Is something burning?"

"Damn," Angie said again as she rushed to the over and took out the scorched cookies. "I forgot the cookies."

A strange expression crossed Chad's face as he looked at them. Angie couldn't read it. "Is something wrong?"

His gaze lingered a moment longer on the burnt remnants. Then he shook his head and continued eating.

Angie slid the cookies off the sheet into the trash. She'd screwed up on the rolls and dessert, but at least Chad seemed to be enjoying the chicken, and Jessica was quietly entertaining herself with cracker crumbs.

It was a start.

Chapter Ten

Another Monday morning and another grumpy start. Eve unrolled the wool muffler wrapped around her throat and opened her all-weather coat as she climbed the stairs to the school. A blue norther had blown in over the weekend, sending temperatures plummeting, and her mood hadn't been far behind.

She'd spent a frustrating Sunday after streaming an erotic movie she planned to share with Brian yesterday afternoon—he much preferred watching porn at her place to football replays with the coaches—only to find out he'd gotten coerced into helping Brenda prepare for the charity lunch coming up the following weekend.

Even the perky desk clerk had looked down this morning. Eve wondered if it had something to do with Molly's on-line guy. Last week she had all but bubbled over about a dinner they'd gone to. Eve shook her head as she unlocked the door to her classroom. She couldn't recall ever having been as trustingly open as Molly was, yet Eve had fallen for every sucker-line her conniving ex handed out. A part of her wanted to warn Molly to be careful. People weren't always who they seemed to be. Yet she hardly knew the girl other than to exchange pleasantries. A butt-insky she was not.

"Hey! Watch where you're going, jerk!"

Eve turned in time to see a student she didn't know glaring at Trey. Trey must have bumped into him, since his thumbs were busily engaged on his cell screen.

He looked up. "Stay out of my way then, *jerk*."

The boy's face turned red. "Who are you calling jerk, asshole?"

Trey's eyes grew darker. "Do you want to say that again?"

"Yeah—"

"*Enough*." Damn it. Eve didn't need a fight breaking out first thing in the morning, and especially not one that involved Trey. "Go inside," she said to him and turned to the other kid. "And you need to watch your language."

The boy scowled at her, and for a moment Eve thought he might start something with her. Trey hadn't moved, either. Damn it again. She really wasn't in the mood for this. "There is nothing for either of you to be upset about. Trey, take your seat." She gave the other student a steady look. "Go to class."

He muttered something Eve couldn't catch, since several of her students swarmed past them at the moment, and by the time they passed, he'd walked off.

Eve sighed. Great way to start the morning. Moving to her desk, she flipped her computer on and watched a series of emails roll up. One caught her eye. It was from Brian. He rarely used her school email address, and she noticed it was from his office as well. Figuring it had to do with Trey, she opened it, only to find Brian asked her to go to Blog-Face.

Eve glanced around the room. Her students were still shuffling in. She slipped her hand inside her purse to engage her cell.

—Were you hot for me yesterday?—

Her eyes popped at the message. She was at school!

—Not now.—

—Why not?—

—You know why not. I've got a class.—

—I wanted to be inside you.—

Was he insane? She couldn't sext now.

—Stop it!—

—K. Just wanted to give you something to think about today.—

—So not fair.—

—I'll make it up to you, babe. Tomorrow night?—

—K. GG.—

—Stay hot and wet.—

Good Lord! Eve disconnected, slipping her cell back into her purse. She could feel steam radiating off her face. Brushing some papers off her desk, she bent over to retrieve them, giving herself a bit of time to recover. Curse the man. His ruse had worked. Moisture was already forming between her legs, and she was totally turned on by the impropriety of the whole thing. Coupled with the frustration from yesterday—the pink bunny had only helped a little bit—she was going to be spending the day hot and bothered. And Brian wouldn't be coming over until tomorrow night. The wait would be torture, which was exactly what he'd intended.

Straightening, Eve smiled. She'd think of something to pay him back.

"What's so funny?" one of the girls asked.

With a start, she realized she was probably grinning like an idiot, and for once, the class was actually sitting at attention. She glanced at the clock. Good grief! The tardy bell had rung five minutes ago.

"Nothing. Just a joke a friend sent," she said. "Let's take out our notes on tone, tint, and hue. We need to review for the test."

Amid the group's grumbling and rustling of papers, Eve noticed Trey watching her with that steady, dark look of his. A corner of his mouth lifted in the quirky way that was half-smile, half-smirk, and he slowly reached for his binder.

****

Molly checked her phone once more before she shoved it back into her purse. Still no message from Chad. Here it was, Monday morning, and she hadn't heard from him since the message he'd sent Thursday morning after their dinner.

Why hadn't he contacted her? Over and over, she'd replayed the events of the dinner in her mind, searching for something she'd said that might have been taken the wrong way. But the evening had been perfect. He'd even *kissed* her—a pleasant tingle resonated through her body at the thought—and he'd *said* he'd had a good time and called her "luv." So why hadn't he blogged her?

Maybe something had happened to him. He could have been in a car accident or something. Waco was almost a two-hour drive on I-35. With the increased big-rig traffic due to Eagle Ford Shale fracking, there were a lot more wrecks. There'd also been a lot of cold rain this weekend, making the roads slick. Maybe even an icy mixture. What if Chad was in a hospital somewhere?

Molly had resisted the urge to Blog-Face him after she'd responded to his message Thursday morning. Mom had taught her women didn't chase men. Still, would she really be *chasing* Chad if she just sent a quick message asking if he was okay? They had met three times, after all.

She waited until Mrs. Wilson swept through on her mission to catch tardy kids and then turned to Joni.

"Can I ask you a question?"

"Fire away."

"Do you ever...um, ever text any of the men you date?"

Joni gave her a quizzical look. "Of course. Who isn't on Blog-Face?"

"I mean...do you ever send a message first?"

"First?"

"Yes, like...if it's been a...a day or so, do you initiate contact?"

"Sure. Why wouldn't I?"

"Um...well, where I come from, the guys usually take the lead."

"You're kidding! Aren't you?" Joni paused. "Oh, my God, you're not kidding. Honey, this is the twenty-first century and this is Big D. If you find a guy attractive, you let him know." Her eyes widened suddenly. "Is this about the one you had dinner with last week?"

Molly was sure her face must be the color of a boiled beet. Her cheeks certainly felt hot enough to have been immersed in hot water. "Um...yes."

Joni gave her a sympathetic look. "How long since you heard from him?"

"Thursday morning."

"After the date? What'd he say?"

"That he had a good time."

Joni arched an eyebrow. "How good of a time?"

"Fantastic! We had a romantic dinner with wine, and I got serenaded, and—"

"I mean—" Joni lowered her voice. "Did you go to bed with him?"

"Did I *what*?" Molly's voice almost squeaked in her

shock. "Of course not!"

"Did he kiss you?"

Molly's face grew hotter. "I really shouldn't say."

Joni rolled her eyes. "I'm not asking for the details here. Just yes or no."

Molly looked down at the counter. Merciful heavens, could faces spontaneously combust from embarrassment? "Yes."

Joni edged her chair closer. "Hey, that's good."

"Yeah, I know." Molly allowed herself a smile. "It *was* good."

"Okay, then, I think I know what the problem is."

"You do?"

"Sure. Here's a guy that's being a gentleman—"

"Yes! Yes, he is."

"—who's taken you out three times, right? *Three* times," she repeated when Molly nodded. "Most guys expect to get a little action—well, actually some *real* action—by the third date."

Molly felt her eyes go round. "You mean…" She dropped to a whisper. "Sex?"

"That's the word. If this guy's not pushing you, he must really like you."

"Do you really think so?"

Joni rolled her eyes again. "Sweetie. We live in a fast-paced world. If this guy is taking his time, he likes you. Maybe he's actually waiting for you to contact him."

Molly felt a glimmer of hope. "You think so?"

"Hey, why not? He's paid for three dates. Maybe he wants to know the pursuit isn't all one-sided. Like I said, this is the twenty-first century. Go ahead and blog him. Just keep it casual."

"Okay, I will!" Molly looked down the hall to make sure Mrs. Wilson wasn't in sight and pulled out her phone. Casual meant no asking why he hadn't blogged. She took a deep breath.

—Hi. Been kind of a bummer weekend with the storm. Hope all's well.—

Molly laid her cell in her lap, under the desk in case Mrs. Wilson made an appearance, and began to organize a stack of papers, trying to keep her mind occupied, but the phone vibrated before she'd even begun. Molly glanced down quickly.

—Hey, luv. Been a super busy weekend. How about a movie Thursday?—

Breathing a giddy sigh of relief, Molly typed back.

—I would "luv" that. See you Thursday.—

Joni gave her a knowing look. "Guess things are all right?"

"Oh, yes! More than all right!" Molly smiled happily. "Things are perfect."

****

Eve glanced at the wall clock for the umpteenth time. The minutes of the final period of the day were passing as slowly as the first trickle of water breaking through an icy creek in springtime. Brian's erotic blog earlier had keep her in a state of semi-arousal most of the day. She needed to get home and sext him back, bunny in hand.

Just as the students were putting up their work, the intercom came on. The placid voice of Mrs. Wilson's secretary filled the room. "Miss O'Connor, please report to the principal's office directly after school."

"Busted!" one of the boys called out, and several girls giggled.

Eve leveled a look at the student and managed not to grit her teeth as she thanked the woman for the message. Damn it, she wanted to get *home*. Mrs. Wilson usually stomped through the halls after school, so what was so important that she would stay in her office?

"What'd you do?" the boy asked, undaunted by her "teacher look."

"I don't know," Eve answered. "Maybe Mrs. Wilson wants to give me a bonus for putting up with silly questions."

"Gotcha!" one of the other students said to him. "That was a good one!"

"Or," Eve continued, making sure her voice sounded playful, "maybe she has another test she wants you guys to take."

There was a group moan as the bell rang, and the students broke for the door. Eve gathered her things, locked the room, and walked toward the office. She was heading straight out as soon as she found out what Mrs. Wilson wanted.

"She's in the conference room," the secretary informed Eve.

The fact that the principal was in the conference room—or "the war room" as most teachers called it—didn't bode well. Eve opened the door to find Mr. Conrad, Mr. Thatcher, and Mrs. Torres already there, along with a sullen-looking Trey, slumped in a chair, sporting a black eye. "What happened?" she asked as she sat down.

Before she got an answer, the door opened again and Brenda walked in, followed by Brian. Eve's breath caught in her throat. The last person she needed to see—in front of a group of people that included his wife and son—was Brian. Her body was already responding to his presence. Her nipples beaded beneath her sweater and warm moisture accumulated between her legs as a slow pulsating began there. Damn it. From the way his eyes darkened when he looked at her, Eve knew Brian was thinking along the same lines as she was.

"Whatever happened?" Brenda asked, moving toward Trey only to have Brian pull her back.

"I'd say it looks like he's been in a fight."

Mrs. Wilson indicated two empty chairs at the end of the table. "Please have a seat." Once they had complied, the principal turned to Eve. "It is my understanding an altercation took place in your classroom this morning."

Heck. Eve had nearly forgotten about that. "It was in the hallway before class. Trey accidently bumped into some kid. They exchanged a few words. Nothing major."

"As you can see, it obviously became something major," Mrs. Wilson replied. "Why didn't you report it?"

Geez. If teachers reported every little incident, they'd need to hire a dozen full-time clerks just to keep up with the paperwork. "I thought I'd handled it. Trey went into my room and the other student took off to his class."

"That sounds reasonable," Brian said.

"So what happened?" Brenda asked Trey.

He shrugged. "Nothing."

"Sit up," Brian said, "and answer your mother."

Trey adjusted himself marginally and shifted his gaze from his father to Eve and then to his mother. "The asshole—"

"Watch your language," Brian said, "and *sit up*."

Trey gave him a surly look, then slowly adjusted his

posture further. "The *jerk* came up to me at lunch and told me to meet him outside after school."

"School had not been dismissed," Mrs. Wilson interrupted. "What were the both of you doing out of class?" Her glance swept the group of teachers. "Students should not be allowed out of classes."

Eve refrained from rolling her eyes, although she noticed John looking at the ceiling, and Irma studying a spot on the carpet. Eve sometimes wondered if administration was connected to the reality of school at all. First, teachers were told they couldn't forbid students from going to the restrooms because of possible medical liabilities, then they were told not to let students out of the classrooms. Which was all probably a moot issue anyway, since anyone planning a fight would simply skip class to begin with.

Brian gestured to his son. "Answer the principal."

"I was on my way to class when the ass—the *jerk*— came up to me."

Brenda folded her hands in her lap. "We've discussed fighting before, Trey. You just should have refused."

Arthur fixed his gaze on her. "It is not quite that easy, Mrs. Caldwell. No one condones fighting, of course, but it's difficult for a teenager to back down." He turned back to Trey. "But there are other ways to handle the situation."

"I agree," Brian added, "and we will deal with this at home. What is our recourse for school?"

"He will be suspended for three days, as will the other student," Mrs. Wilson answered. "If Trey gets into another fight, we'll have no choice but to send him to the Alternative Education Center."

Brian glanced at Brenda. "And there is always the boot camp."

"I believe you said we'd discuss this at home," she replied.

"You are free to leave," Mrs. Wilson said, "but I need for Trey's teachers to stay. I want a word with them."

Eve bit back a groan. The principal could be a real battle-ax once she got into warrior mode. She'd make sure the teachers felt as much to blame for the fight as the kids. Eve dared a glance at Brian as he turned to leave.

A corner of his mouth lifted and he raised a brow in question.

Eve felt her face warm as heat washed over her body. She knew what he was silently asking. Subtly, she inclined her head.

Blog-Face sex was going to be good tonight.

****

"Sorry I didn't blog you last night," Brian told Eve the next evening as he lifted her naked body over his. "Things got a little heated at home, and not in the right way."

"Talk later," Eve muttered as she leaned over him, brushing his bare chest with her taut nipples, then raising to let her breasts sway a tantalizing few inches from his lips. Running her fingers through his hair, she pressed his head to the pillow and continued to tease by eluding his eager mouth.

"Come on, babe. Let me taste."

"Mmmm." Eve slid back, raising her bottom and lowering her breasts to create delicious friction again as she shifted her ribs from side to side across Brian's chest.

"Maybe not yet."

"Witch."

Eve laughed, straddling him.

Brian bucked beneath her. "Take it, babe."

"In a little while. You had me hot and bothered most of yesterday. I think I'll just prolong your torture a little more."

He growled, his hands circling her waist as he flipped her over, mounting her in one deft stroke as his thighs spread her legs wide. "I don't think so."

Eve gasped as he plunged fully inside her. "I wanted to ride you."

"You took too long." Brian kneaded her breasts with his palms while his fingers and thumbs tugged at her nipples. "Come for me."

Eve arched into his hands, her breathing shallow as he thrust hard and fast. Strong contractions undulated inside her core. She screamed as her body convulsed and shattered. With a final grunt, Brian spilled himself into her.

For several minutes they lay still, bodies sleek with sweat. Then Brian rolled over and sat up, reaching for his jeans.

"Leaving so soon?"

"Sorry, babe. I have to."

Eve arched and stretched, bringing her arms over her head to rest on the pillow. "Sure I can't change your mind?"

He glanced at her naked body and grinned. "You really are a witch, aren't you?"

"Ummm. Maybe."

Putting on his shirt, he shook his head. "I wish I could stay. Things are in turmoil at the house over what happened yesterday at school."

Eve swung her legs over the bed and sat up, reaching for a black silk robe. "If I'd known the matter wasn't settled, I would have done more to put a stop to it."

"Probably nothing you could do. Boys will be boys."

"Trey doesn't strike me as a fighter, though. Did he hurt the other kid?"

Brian shrugged. "He says he knocked the other kid out. He's probably just bragging though."

"I didn't hear any rumors at school," Eve said as she walked Brian to the door. "Most of the time, it's all kids can talk about. I'll definitely be more watchful when Trey returns. The Alternate School isn't that great a place."

"I still think the kid needs boot camp," Brian said and leaned down to give Eve a kiss, "which is one more reason I have to get home. I took away his electronics for the week, and I don't want Brenda giving them back in a weak moment."

Eve smiled. "Your wife doesn't exactly come across as weak."

"You got that right. Maybe I should have said she's more like a she-bear with one cub when it comes to Trey."

"That's not an image I like either." Eve smiled. "I hear bears are territorial."

Brian laughed and opened the door. "Don't worry. I'm not her cub."

Eve's smile faded as she shut the door. She didn't like getting involved in students' personal lives, but she would have to keep an eye on Trey. Brenda Caldwell was one complication she didn't need.

Chapter Twelve

Seducing a virgin took as much strategy as planning a game. The only difference was Chad's offensive couldn't be forceful enough for Molly to become defensive—a challenge he found quite interesting and intriguing.

As he rang Molly's doorbell Thursday night, he thought about the movie he'd chosen for them to see. He didn't think Molly was the type to enjoy a shoot-'em-up-and-explode-everything-else action flick, and he'd pretty much resigned himself to a rom-com, when he'd Googled indie theatres. To his surprise, there was one on the North Side that was showing the old Beatles classic *Hard Day's Night*. Given her affinity for retro-Brit, he couldn't have asked for a better choice. And it started at seven o'clock, which meant he'd be home by ten. Early enough that Angie wouldn't raise a stink, especially since he'd been home every evening this week.

Strategy.

Molly opened the door with a big smile. "I got your message you'd be early."

"Yeah, a surprise. It's a slight change in plans, but I think you'll approve."

She picked up her purse from a nearby chair. "I love surprises! What is it?"

"I found an indie that's showing *Hard Day's Night*—"

"Oooh!" Molly exclaimed and threw her arms around his neck. "How wonderful!"

Chad wrapped his arms around her waist and hugged her briefly before stepping back. Play One executed smoothly—even better than he expected, but he didn't want Molly to think he'd take advantage. At least, not yet. He found himself enjoying drawing out this seduction, possibly because he and Angie had actually managed to have sex twice over the weekend without the baby crying, and he was somewhat satiated. "I thought you might say that. Shall we go?"

Molly kept up a constant chatter about the Beatles on their drive to the theatre. "Gran was in the ninth grade when the Beatles first came to the States. She told me about seeing them on the Ed Sullivan show, although there was so much screaming she could hardly hear the music."

"Kind of like the boy bands today, huh? All the 'tweens screech at them."

"Except the Beatles were already in their twenties when they became famous," Molly replied. "Gran said she begged to go to one of their concerts, but her mother said no. They still squabble about that, although in a teasing way."

Chad tried to remember what he recalled about the group besides their hair—and that was just from pictures. His grandmother hadn't cared for rock—British or otherwise. He'd always felt like the odd-boy-out when the other kids would discuss current songs on their latest CDs.

"Two of them are still performing. Maybe your grandmother could still go."

Molly giggled. "She did a few years ago. I don't

think it was quite the same."

"Probably not, since all those guys are now senior citizens."

Molly nodded. "True, but the music is still good. I think that's what my gran likes best. The music lives on."

"You're probably right. To survive in the entertainment business for more than a few years—let alone decades—says something." He turned into the parking lot of the theatre. "Here we are."

"Oh, look! They've even got old posters!"

Chad glanced at them as they went inside. At least he'd remembered the moppy hair right. The guys looked really young. Hell, they *were* young. At thirty, he was probably a good five years older than any of them had been when they'd made the movie back then—a rather brittle reminder that he was aging too.

At least he didn't have trouble picking up women—yet. Whoever his father had been, he must have had good genes. Even Eve teased Chad about looking like a Greek god, although the few times he'd offered to make her feel like a goddess, she'd turned him down. Probably smart. She was the one woman he counted as a real friend, not clingy and not demanding.

Chad looked sideways at Molly as they took their seats in the darkened theatre. He'd have to be careful with this one. Her family sounded close-knit, which meant she'd have expectations. Everything about her screamed "relationship," and given the fact that she worked at Deer Hill, he probably should have dropped her like a hot frying pan before he found himself engulfed in fire. But damn it, he'd never had a virgin.

He put his arm around her, letting his hand rest lightly on her shoulder. Molly inhaled sharply and then leaned toward him. He lightly massaged her upper arm, not taking the movement further. She smiled up at him as the movie began. He returned the smile. Oh, yeah, taking this slow and easy was going to be well worth the reward.

****

"Would you like to come in?" Molly asked as Chad walked her to her apartment after the movie.

"Sure, for a little while."

Chad was such a gentleman, Molly reflected as she opened the door and turned on a lamp in the small living room. She didn't have enough experience dating—she'd known Tommy forever—but she wasn't sure it was appropriate to ask a man she hadn't been seeing that often into her place after a date. Nor was she sure how to get him to leave without being rude. But Chad had already solved that issue by saying "for a little while" as though he'd read her mind. Molly relaxed. He truly was a gentleman.

"Please have a seat," Molly said. Her stomach fluttered as Chad chose the sofa, and then she chided herself silently. Where had she expected him to sit? Besides, if she wanted to be honest with herself, she had liked having his arm around her at the movie. "Would you like something to drink?"

"A beer, if you have it."

"Of course." Molly went to her tiny kitchen, proud that she'd stocked beer. Even though she didn't drink much, she'd bought several different kinds of hard liquor as well when she moved to Dallas. Having a "bar" for guests made her feel somewhat sophisticated. Considering Chad was her first real guest, if she didn't count Joni dropping over, Molly decided she'd celebrate with a glass of wine herself.

She carried the beverages into the living room and took a seat beside Chad, careful to leave a little room. She didn't want him to think she was one of those women who chased men blatantly.

"Nice job decorating," Chad said. "You've got some interesting stuff."

"They're just some things from home," Molly answered, secretly pleased. "This old pine furniture came from my great-grandfather's ranch house, and that quilt—" Molly pointed to the blanket neatly folder over a wooden rocker "—my great-grandmother made. I'm so lucky to have it."

"Are both your great-grandparents still alive?"

"Yes, but since they're in their nineties, Daddy convinced them to come live with him and my mom. It's why I got their furniture." Molly gestured to a wall with an arrangement of family photos. "And some of their pictures."

Chad gave her an odd look. "You sound pretty close to your family."

"I am. What about you?"

He paused. "My parents are gone. Mostly, my grandmother raised me."

"Is she still alive?"

"Yes. She lives in Waco."

"Does she live with you?"

A perplexed look crossed his face and then it cleared. "No. She's in an assisted living place there. I, er, rent a place not far away." Chad set the beer down and took Molly's arm, tugging her closer. "Enough about families. I had a nice time tonight."

Maybe the half glass of wine she'd had helped, but

Molly felt very comfortable snuggling into the circle of his embrace. Like at the theatre, his hand gently stroked her arm. She tilted her face upward to speak and then lost her train of thought as Chad's mouth descended on hers.

This kiss was nothing like the other. No brushing of lips, no light teasing. His lips were firm against hers, moving insistently, molding her mouth to his, the pressure pleasantly titillating. With a small sigh of contentment, Molly's lips parted, and then she stiffened in shock as Chad's tongue filled her.

"Relax," he whispered, gliding his tongue along her lower lip and then teasing her with partial entry. "This is where it gets to be fun, luv."

Being enveloped in his embrace *did* feel good. Molly felt safe and warm. Tentatively, she let her tongue touch his. A low moan emanated from Chad's throat and he pulled her closer, plundering more fully. Once she got used to the feel of him inside her mouth, Molly realized she quite liked the texture and taste. Her tongue tangled with his, and Chad moaned again, his hand sliding to caress the side of her breast, his thumb grazing the hardened tip beneath her bra. Molly gasped again and tried to pull back, but Chad held her tight.

"It's okay, luv. I won't go any further than this. Just tell me if you like it."

Like it? Molly's senses were overwhelmed. Strange, tingling sensations coursed through her body as Chad slowly kneaded her breast. It felt suddenly heavy, her nipple on fire. Muscles contracted low in her belly and warm wetness gushed between her thighs. She struggled for air as he deepened their kiss. She began to tremble and clung to him, knowing she should tell him to stop, yet not wanting the intense feelings to stop.

As though he read her mind, Chad's hand slowed and he broke off their kiss. "I think I'd better leave before I lose control," he said, his voice husky.

Molly wasn't sure what control he was talking about, but as the sensations began to wane, her sensibility returned. Good heavens! What had nearly happened? Then she realized. Her breath shuddered. So this was what being turned on felt like. She felt her face heat and looked down. "Yes, I guess you should go."

Chad lifted her chin with a finger and brushed a kiss against her forehead. "Don't be embarrassed. It's natural, and it felt good."

Molly nodded, unable to speak.

Chad stood and made his way to the door. "I'll be in touch, luv."

She nodded again, still trying to register all the emotions racing through her brain. What would have happened if he'd not stopped? Would she have...*could* she have... ? She needed time to think. Thank goodness Chad had stopped, since she obviously didn't have the willpower to do so.

He was such a gentleman.

****

Eve was removing mail from her pigeonhole Friday morning when she heard Molly squeal. Turning quickly, Eve almost bumped into Arthur, who had been putting flyers in other boxes.

Joni giggled and looked heavenward. "She just got a sext from her on-line hottie."

Eve resisted commenting, since the desk clerk had turned garnet red. She was tempted to say she could relate, given that Brian had done the same thing to her on Monday, but somehow she didn't think Molly was quite ready to discuss sexting in any context. Besides, there were other people about.

Eve glanced at Arthur, who had furrowed his brows, and she raised her own. "You object to sexting?"

He shrugged. "Never tried it."

Before she could say more, Joni cut in. "What *else* did the guy say?"

Molly's face was still ruby-pink, but she smiled happily, her eyes lighting. Eve felt a twinge of envy—had she ever been that besotted over a man? She couldn't recall.

"He told me—in Beatle song titles—what a wonderful time he had last night."

Arthur stepped closer. "Beatle song titles?"

"Yes." Molly smiled up at him. "My gran was crazy about all the British groups. I kind of grew up on their music."

Joni poked her. "So tell us."

Molly looked down at her message and giggled. "*Yesterday*, I was a *Nowhere Man*, but now *I Feel Fine* because *Baby, It's You. Please Please Me*. All you have to do is *Act Naturally*." She blushed again at the last title.

"That's pretty impressive," Arthur said.

"Or pretty slick. Sorry," Eve said when three pairs of eyes turned to her. "Call me cynical. You just have to be careful not to believe everything a guy says on-line. Most of it's blarney anyway."

"I don't think it's blarney," Molly said.

"Interesting word," Arthur interjected, probably to neutralize the situation and tilted his head at Eve with an amused look. "I can't believe someone named O'Connor would not have an affinity for blarney."

"Rubbish. I've been to Ireland and seen the castle.

Anyone who wants to hang backwards over a battlement to kiss a dirty stone is a complete fool."

"Tsk, tsk," Arthur replied. "Such cynicism." He turned back to Molly. "Actually, the legend—or legends—are rather romantic."

Molly's eyes grew round. "Really?"

"Yes," he said, ignoring Eve's derisive sigh. "Blarney Castle—or *Cloch na Blarnan* in Gaelic—dates to the fifteenth century and sits a few kilometers from Cork, Ireland. Do you want to hear the rest?"

"Yes!" Joni and Molly replied in unison while Eve shook her head.

Arthur grinned at them. "The most popular legend tells of the owner, Cormac Laidir MacCarthy, being involved in a lawsuit—some tales say with Elizabeth the First. When he prayed to the goddess Cliodna, he was told in a vision to kiss the first stone he saw in the morning and he would win his lawsuit. Another story relates that Robert the Bruce gave Cormac the Blarney Stone in recognition of his support of Bannockburn. Anyway, the grateful MacCarthy had the bluestone placed in a parapet beneath the battlements—which, as Miss O'Connor indicated, are rather treacherous."

"I think you're a bit full of blarney too, Mr. Conrad." Eve laughed, in spite of herself. "Are you sure you aren't Irish?"

"Afraid not," he replied and then smiled at Molly. "If you want a more recent legend, Texas Tech in Lubbock claims to have a piece of the Blarney Stone in front of their engineering department building. How's that for blarney?"

"Oh, geez. Where did you dig that up?"

Arthur held up his hands. "Supposedly, it's true."

Eve shook her head again and looked at Molly as the tardy bell rang. "See? This is exactly what I mean. You just can't believe everything you hear."

Molly returned her smile, but her eyes were solemn. "Maybe, but I still think my message is romantic."

Eve felt the twinge of envy flit through her mind again. She'd taken off—and thrown away—her rose-colored glasses long ago. "Good for you, then. I'm sorry I said anything." As she left to go to class, she just hoped whoever this guy was that he was taking Molly for a long, winding ride.

Chapter Thirteen

Eve felt like she was wearing a rehabilitative boot on each foot as she parked her car at the Hilton Anatole Saturday and reluctantly walked toward the lobby. She had never been fond of attending charitable events—not that she didn't donate to charity, she did—but she just didn't like the social aspect of having to engage in polite, meaningless conversation with people she didn't know. Certainly, the expensive, complimentary tickets for this lunch could have been put to better use.

But the real reason she dreaded this particular luncheon—and she knew it—was spending more time with Brenda Caldwell.

Damn it. Eve did not want to socialize with Brian's wife. Eve hadn't given much thought to what kind of marriage they had. Quite the opposite. The less she knew about Brian's family life, the better. Mentally, it allowed her to compartmentalize her own life. Sex fit neatly into its own category. When Eve was with Brian, that was all that mattered—just the two of them. When he went home, what he did was his business.

The plan had worked for nearly a year, until Trey transferred to Deer Hill. Heck, Eve hadn't even known the kid's name. Hadn't asked. Brian hadn't been inclined to mention either of his kids either. Their world was a cozy cocoon of sensual, sexy fantasies, separated from the world of reality.

Damn it.

"Why so glum?" Irma Torres asked as she approached the front doors the same time as Eve. "I hear the Anatole has an excellent chef. Lunch should be fabulous."

"I'll bet it's chicken," Eve replied and then forced a smile. No need to take out her ire on another teacher. "Maybe the chef can work a miracle and make it taste like lobster or something."

"Actually, I think lobster is on the menu," Irma replied.

"You're kidding."

"No. Mr. Thatcher called to find out." Irma grinned. "I don't think he wanted chicken either."

"I'm sure he and Arthur would both prefer a good ribeye," Eve answered, her mood beginning to lighten when she saw the teachers had all been assigned the same table. Maybe she would have nothing to do with Brenda other than to say thank you when she left.

Arthur stood as they approached and pulled out two chairs. Irma beamed at him and Eve arched a brow, tempted to make a remark about chivalry not being dead, but decided against it. Some men were naturally nice guys, and she didn't need to be snappish about it just because her temper was still on edge. "Thanks."

"Anytime," he replied and sat down, only to spring up again when Mrs. Wilson approached and he repeated the gesture.

Eve smiled, in spite of her edginess. Molly had mentioned what a gentleman her new boyfriend was— maybe this was a developing trend.

A waiter appeared with a bottle of chilled Chardonnay and began filling their glasses. Irma caught her eye and Eve smiled again. "You're right. This isn't bad."

"I knew you'd change your mind," Irma said.

Eve's elation—or the beginning of it—was short-lived. Brenda glided over to them in a subtle cloud of expensive perfume, wearing a simple sheath of peach silk, set off by a single strand of pearls at her throat.

"I'm so glad everyone could attend."

As if they had a choice. Mrs. Wilson would have been hellish to deal with if anyone had stayed home. As it was, she was fawning over the decorations and the wine.

Brenda laughed, the sound as muted as a wind chime in a zephyr breeze. "Since the guests are invited to visit the silent auction before luncheon is served, wine always helps increase the bidding."

"Of course," Mrs. Wilson said. "We'd be delighted to partake."

She pushed back her chair, causing Arthur to stand again, this time along with John. Eve stifled a laugh of her own. Maybe chivalry was indeed becoming a trend. She had never noticed either of the guys being overly polite before, but then, at school everyone was always in a hurry.

As Eve got up, she looked over at Brenda. "I noticed Trey wasn't in school yesterday. His suspension was over on Thursday."

"Yes, but his eye is all sorts of horrible colors. Since school's out for Thanksgiving this week, I thought I'd just keep him home until after the holiday. Thank you for asking, though."

"Sure." Eve followed the other teachers over to the tables that held the various items for the auction. She would bet that Brian hadn't approved the decision to keep Trey at home an extra day. A black eye was really no excuse—

Eve stopped abruptly. Why in the world did she care? It wasn't her business what Brian and Brenda did regarding their son. Dear God. What was wrong with her?

****

"Metro played a great game today," Brian said to Chad as they took seats at the counter of a local corner bar late Saturday afternoon. "No Hail Marys this time."

"Yeah, it felt good to be ahead by a solid lead," Chad replied and then grinned. "But man, I'd love to see a last-minute ninety-yard run like Auburn did a while back."

"That was one for the record books, for sure."

"It was a moment in *history*. We'll probably never see something like that again, not even in the Super Bowl."

Brian nodded, glad that Chad's enthusiasm over football hadn't waned like his had over the past couple of years. He still liked the sport, but being sequestered in an office handling paperwork and finances gave him a different perspective. So did the political maneuvering he constantly had to do to encourage alumni to support not only football but also athletics in general—and he was always competing for those dwindling funds with the Science and Technology departments, to say nothing of the Fine Arts programs. To him, football was no longer a testosterone-overloaded game of roughing up the opponents. When he'd been on the field, winning was a euphoric high—now winning was all that mattered, to the Board of Regents, at least. Still, active coaches had to keep that competitive edge. Chad demonstrated it in spades.

And that competitive edge rolled over into Chad's personal life as well. "Are you going to celebrate with your girlfriend or your wife tonight?"

"Angie. She's gotten this crazy idea of learning to cook."

Brian swirled his Scotch. "Is that a bad thing?"

"Depends on if you like things scorched or half-raw." Chad chugged some beer and set the mug down. "Actually, some of the stuff isn't too bad. At least, it's not always spaghetti or pizza."

"That's good to hear, especially since Angie invited Brenda and me to your place for Thanksgiving next week."

"She did *what*?"

Brian set his glass down. "Apparently, she's been getting entertaining tips from my wife and now wants to demonstrate her skills."

"In that case, you'd better eat a full meal before you come over."

Brian laughed. "It can't be that bad."

Chad looked skeptical. "She's barely managed casseroles. I can't imagine her roasting a turkey, let alone getting all the trimmings done."

"Don't worry about it. There are places that provide pre-cooked turkeys. If Brenda is involved, she'll probably have all the side dishes ordered and delivered."

"That would be a relief. At least, no one will come down with food poisoning."

"Well, my wife likes being in charge and she likes entertaining, so I think you can rest easy about everything." And, with any luck, keeping Brenda occupied with helping Angie might give Brian a time to slip away and do a little sexting with Eve. She never expected him to show up on a holiday, but he still liked to stay in touch—and building sexual tension for their next encounter. He glanced over at Chad.

"Did you have to make an excuse to your girlfriend?"

"Nope. Got lucky. She's going to the Hill Country to see her folks next week. She thinks I'm visiting my elderly grandmother in Waco."

"In Waco?"

"Yeah. That's where I supposedly live too. It's easier handling an affair if you're not available on a regular basis."

Brian shook his head. "One of these days, you're going to get caught."

"Doubtful, man. I use an alias, my 'job' is somewhat sports-related, and I travel on business, which accounts for my not being around. It's foolproof."

"I hope you're right." To Brian, it seemed like a lot of work. His previous affairs—if he could actually call them that—mainly had been out-of-town one-nighters when he was still coaching. Eve had been a godsend when he'd met her last year. The perfect mistress—sexual, intelligent, and wanting no commitments. And he didn't have to lie to her. She knew his circumstances. Maybe a little too well, as of late.

Chad set his empty mug on the counter and stood. "Better go. Maybe I can prevent another casserole from being charred to a crisp."

Brian stood too. "I'm leaving too. Brenda will be back from the luncheon by now, and I want to find out how it went."

"The one Eve was invited to?" Chad asked.

"Yeah."

Chad shook his head. "You're the one who needs to be careful. There'll be hell to pay if Brenda ever finds out."

He was right, although probably not for the reasons Chad was thinking. Brian felt a moment of apprehension, but he pushed it aside. "I've got it covered."

****

The acrid smell of smoke filled the hallway when Chad let himself into his house. Evidently, another of Angie's dinners had not made it through the cooking process. He sighed. At this point, he was ready to tell her just to go back to spaghetti and pizza, but she seemed determined to cook, although why, he didn't know. They'd gotten through five years of marriage with no attempt at culinary skills.

He found Angie in the kitchen standing over the sink, scraping burnt skin off something that might have been part of a chicken. On the counter stood a dish that might have been potatoes of some sort, although it was hard to tell since the top layer was blackened as well.

Jessica was in her highchair, squealing as she stuck her fingers in a cereal bowl and swirled milk everywhere. When she saw Chad, she shrieked even louder and hurled cereal in his direction. He ducked as the bits flew past his head. The kid did have a good throwing arm. Too bad she wasn't a boy.

Angie turned around. "You're home early!"

Chad glanced at the attempts of dinner. "I'd say I'm late."

Angie followed his gaze. "Oh, that. It'll be fine when I get the black stuff off." She plunked the piece of chicken on a platter and set in on the table. "I was making scalloped potatoes, but I turned the oven on too high. Have a seat."

Cautiously, Chad eyed his daughter, judging the distance, and took a seat at the other end of the kitchen table. He knew better than to take the bowl away. Jessica had a healthy set of lungs that equaled her athletic ability. Enduring a screaming child would be the finishing touch to what looked like an inedible meal. He should have gotten a burger before he came home.

Angie took a salad out of the fridge that looked like no harm had been done to it, although how anyone could ruin lettuce and tomato would be hard to figure. Chad took a healthy portion of it, sliced a few slivers of the toughened meat, and by-passed the potatoes. In contrast, Angie helped herself to large portions.

"I think I'm getting better at this."

Chad choked and reached for the water glass. Angie didn't exactly run on high-wattage, but had she become dimwitted since she was staying home more? True, her cooking no longer set off the smoke alarm, but then, he hadn't checked the batteries lately. He couldn't remember a single meal in her attempts over the past week that hadn't had the consistency of cracked leather. "Why did you suddenly decide you wanted to cook? I've never asked you to."

"Oh, I know. You've been really sweet. I just decided, since I quit full-time work this summer, that I'd like to become more of a homemaker."

Chad took another swallow of water, not trusting himself to down a bite of anything. Angie's "homemaking" skills hardly rated above her cooking skills. Dirty dishes stayed stacked in the sink. Magazines and toys were scattered throughout the living room, and the bedroom was cluttered with discarded clothes that should have found the laundry bin but got launched elsewhere.

And Angie was actually thinking about *entertaining*?

"Well, perhaps you should concentrate on just one thing at a time. Keep it simple. I'm wondering if it's such a good idea to have Brian and Brenda over for Thanksgiving."

"Nonsense. Brenda said she'd help. Everything will be fine."

Chad stared at Angie in disbelief. Did his wife actually think she could pull this off? Their place looked like a disaster, they had a kid who'd given new meaning to the phrase "Terrible Twos," and how could they serve food just this side of being incinerated?

"The holiday is a big undertaking. Maybe we should just settle for a small dinner some other time?"

Angie's lower lip protruded. It was a gesture Chad used to find sexy, since it meant she wasn't pleased and wanted to be pampered—and his idea of pampering involved eventual removal of her clothing. Heck, he used to tease her just to get her to pout, and one thing would lead to another. Angie had been fun before the baby came, but she no longer seemed interested in such indulgences. Now the gesture meant she was getting ready to argue.

"Fine," he said and stood abruptly before she could get started. "We'll do things your way." He added his dishes to the ones already in the sink. "Just don't blame me if it doesn't go well. I'll be in my office."

Once there, he switched on the computer. Molly had left for her parents' place this morning, but she'd have her cell. Chad sat back in his chair, waiting for the computer to come to life, envisioning what her holiday would be like. He knew her family was close. From her great-grandparents' knotty pine furniture in her apartment—which was dust and clutter free, yet had a warm, welcoming feel—he could imagine a ranch house set on acreage surrounded by mesquite trees, sage brush, and maybe prickly-pear cactus. A huge fireplace in the main room would emit crackling flames from scrub oak. The succulent aroma of roasting turkey would fill the area, as would the savory scents of pumpkin and pecan pies.

Chad shook his head as the Blog-Face screen popped up. Hell, the next thing he'd be doing is imagining a horse-drawn sleigh through snowy woods. What was it about Molly that made him think about traditions that didn't even exist outside of movies and songs? People didn't really gather round the table spouting feelings of good cheer.

He entered his password.

—Hey, luv. Hope you had a safe trip.—

A few seconds later, her reply came.

—Arrived fine. You're sweet to ask.—

—You're the one who's sweet.—

—Thank you, Sir Galahad. (giggle) Getting ready to go to Musikfest.—

—Musikfest?—

—It's a concert with German music and German Christmas carols.—

—Have fun then. Miss you.—

—Miss you too. Talk later.—

Chad signed off . Apparently, some traditions were followed after all. Briefly, he wondered what it would be like to be a part of a family like that. Then he shrugged off the feeling. If he wasn't careful, he'd end up getting emotionally involved. A problem he definitely did not need. He hesitated, then clicked on Brian's name in his BF account.

—If you see a florist invoice on my next expense report, chalk it off to Thanksgiving entertaining here. We'll talk football to make it legit.—

—No problem. Angie will probably appreciate the gesture.—

Chad logged off without responding. He could pick up something at the local grocery store for the house. The flower arrangement he had in mind would be waiting for Molly when she returned.

Playing the gallant knight was kind of fun.

****

Angie removed the cereal bowl from Jessica's tray and sopped up the spilt milk. Wiping her daughter's face with a napkin, Angie also removed the bib, thankful it had caught the rest of the mess. She knew she needed to reinforce using a spoon properly, but Chad hated it when the baby started crying, and Angie knew Jessica would.

"Down!"

"Not yet, sweetie. Mommy has to do the dishes."

"Down!"

"In just a little while."

Jessica started kicking the legs of her highchair, causing it to sway. Angie rushed over to steady it. "Stop that."

"Down!"

Angie sighed and picked her child up. All the parenting books said to be firm and consistent, but in another minute, Jessica would be having a tantrum. Her screaming always annoyed Chad, and Angie was too tired to pacify both of them. She carried Jessica into the living room and set her on the sofa along with her favorite toys.

"Stay here until I can straighten up a few things, okay? Then Mommy will come and play with you. Can you be a good girl?"

Jessica looked at her with big, blue eyes and smiled like a cherub. Angie brushed back her hair, gave her a kiss, and hurried back to the kitchen. She piled the dishes into one side of the sink to wash later, dumped the leftover potatoes into the garbage disposal, and ran water into the casserole to loosen the burnt food around the rim.

At least there wasn't as much of the charred remains around the edges of the dish this time. She really was getting the hang of cooking. The chicken had been a little dry, but that was better than her first attempt, when it hadn't cooked through. The last batch of grocery cookie dough had turned out pretty well too.

The lessons with Brenda were paying off. Angie knew she wasn't quite ready to take on an entire Thanksgiving dinner, but she wanted so much to show Chad she was capable of being a good homemaker. When she'd mentioned it to Brenda, a brief expression of surprise had flitted over the other woman's face, but then she'd smiled and said something about circling the wagons. Whatever that meant. Brenda had assured her she would help.

Angie dried her hands and went back to the living room to find the sofa empty. A soft giggle drew her attention to the hallway where Jessica was opening the door to Chad's study. Angie rushed down the hall. "No, no, sweetie. Don't go in. Daddy doesn't like being disturbed."

Too late, she reached the door just as Jessica pushed it open. Startled, Chad looked up from his computer as his daughter ran in.

He caught the grimy little hands that Angie had forgotten to wipe clean and held the child at a distance, frowning at Angie. "I've asked you to keep Jessica out of here because of all the electronics."

"I know. I was trying to clean up," Angie said as she approached to pick Jessica up and then glanced at the laptop. "Who are you Blog Facing?"

Chad's frown deepened and he semi-closed the lid. "I just sent a message to Eve. Brian mentioned something about Trey this afternoon, and I thought Eve should know."

"Oh. Well, I won't bother you. It's almost time for Jessica's bedtime. Do you want to watch a movie when I get her settled?"

He fingered the laptop's lid. "Sure."

Angie hid her surprise as she left the room. Usually, Chad didn't care to watch movies. It would be nice to spend Saturday night curled up on the couch with him.

As she got Jessica ready for bed, Angie thought about Eve. She knew Eve and Chad had been friends since high school, although Angie had only met Eve once. Chad had said something about a nasty divorce last year. Angie always felt sorry for women who divorced and had to live alone. Eve didn't have any children, either, which made it even worse. Angie tucked her daughter into bed and then paused outside the door as a thought struck her.

Eve was one of Trey's teachers. All the Caldwells

would be coming to Thanksgiving dinner. Why not invite Eve too? Angie smiled all the way down the hall. Eve would probably enjoy getting to know one of her students away from school.

Chapter Fourteen

"Mmmm, that turkey roasting smells heavenly!" Molly said as she walked into her mother's kitchen Thanksgiving morning. Her great-grandparents were enjoying hot chocolate at the kitchen table. "That smells good!" She gave each a hug and turned back to her mother. "What can I do to help?"

"I think everything is under control."

"Gran, can I help with the ambrosia salad?"

"Don't even think she'd let you," Molly's grandfather said with a twinkle in his eye. "She has 'secret' ingredients, you know."

"As if you haven't watched me make this salad every year for nearly forty years," her grandmother shot back with an affectionate smile.

Molly's dad slid a bowl of walnuts toward her. "You can shell these. I *know* they go in the salad." He picked through another bowl of chestnuts. "Then you can help me decide which of these will have the most 'pop' when we roast them later in front of the fire."

Molly laughed. "That's a Christmas tradition, not Thanksgiving."

"Well, seeing as how you moved to the big city and all, we thought we'd get a jump start on the season while you're here," Grandpa said.

Molly gave him a hug. "Don't worry. I'll be home for Christmas."

"Sounds like a song we know," her mother said. "I think I have an Elvis CD."

"No Christmas carols before we eat the turkey," her dad replied, trying to look stern. "You always complain the decorations are out in the stores too early."

"That's true," Gran said as she sliced some marshmallows, "and now the retailers are making their poor workers come in on Thanksgiving Day to open. It's a crime, I tell you."

"I'm just glad the school district let us off for the entire week," Molly said as she picked up the nutcracker. "I've missed you guys."

Molly's mom looked up from the green bean casserole she was putting together. "We've missed you too, honey."

"How are things going up there in Dallas?" her dad asked.

"Just great! I like my job, and I've made some good friends amongst the teachers."

"Any gentlemen friends?' Gran inquired with a wink.

Molly's face heated and she hoped she wasn't blushing. She wanted to tell them all about Chad, but how much should she say?

Her father raised a questioning eyebrow. "*Is* there someone you've met?"

She hesitated and then smiled. "Well, I did meet someone."

Four pairs of hands stilled in their tasks and four pairs of eyes turned to her. Her mother spoke first. "Tell us, dear."

"His name is Chad. He's a marketing executive who travels a lot."

Her father gave her a level look. "How did you meet him?"

"Ah…on-line."

"Through one of those dating services?"

"Is that safe?" Molly's great-grandmother interrupted as she set her cup down. "You hear all kinds of things these days."

"It's safe," Molly said hurriedly. "It's actually part of Blog-Face, but it has all kinds of privacy settings once you connect."

"But how much do you know about his background?" her mother asked.

"There's a profile page that has all the information. If a person likes what he or she sees, they click on a 'Getting To Know You' link and you can chat back and forth without giving your last names or anything."

Her great-grandfather snorted. "This newfangled computer stuff is for the birds. Can't tell anything about a person playing on a computer. People need to meet in person."

"Well, we did meet in person. Don't worry," Molly added as both of her father's eyebrows rose. "My friend, Joni, told me what to do. Chad and I met in a public place, and I drove myself."

"But he could have followed you home," her dad said. "I don't want you taking any chances with strangers."

Molly's face flamed again as she remembered her last date with Chad and what happened when he'd taken her home. Just recalling his kiss—and where his hands had been—caused delightful shivers to slide down her spine. Chad could follow her home anytime—not that she could tell her parents that. "He's really very nice,

Dad. He is a real gentleman who treats me like a lady." Molly wasn't sure if ladies actually reacted like she had to Chad's touch, but that was not something that needed to be mentioned either.

"Tommy's a gentleman too, and a good solid boy to settle down with," her grandfather intervened. "He's been asking about you. Nothing wrong with him either."

"Of course there isn't," Molly replied, "but Tommy and I've known each other since grade school. We're friends." She looked to her mother for understanding. "I feel more like his sister than a girlfriend."

Her mother smiled and nodded. "You need a chance to spread your wings a bit." She looked at her husband. "Would you check the turkey? I never can tell when it's the right temperature."

Molly hid a smile. Mom always knew how to get Dad distracted. Just mention food. Still, she was grateful for the intervention. There were questions she couldn't answer and others she didn't want to.

At least, not yet. Maybe soon.

This was turning out to be the best Thanksgiving ever. She was with her family, and Chad had sent her a message earlier, saying he'd have a surprise for her when she returned. Molly could hardly wait to find out what it was—she loved surprises.

****

This had to be Eve's worst nightmare. Why in the world had she ever let herself be persuaded to have Thanksgiving at Chad and Angie's house? She didn't even care for the holidays—even though this was Friday because of the college football schedule—because of all the forced cheerfulness everyone was supposed to feel.

Chad had been surprised to see her when she rang

the bell earlier, wine bottle in one hand and his favorite beer in the other. Apparently, Angie had not told him she'd invited Eve to come over. She'd also neglected to mention that the Caldwells would be here. Eve hated surprises.

Spending a holiday with Brian and Brenda and their son was *so* what Eve did *not* need. All the tidy compartments that she regulated parts of her life to were cracking apart. A sexual affair with a married man was supposed to be just that and nothing more. The wife and kids were supposed to exist—like digital data—in a cloud-like place. Certainly, they weren't supposed to manifest in flesh and blood in front of her where she had to interact with them. Everything had been just fine for almost a year—until her life got complicated when Trey enrolled in her class.

He was slouched in an armchair directly across from the one Eve had chosen, which gave him the opportunity to watch her without it seeming intentional. She would have moved out of his line of vision, but the only other place to sit was on the sofa, and Brian was there. Eve wasn't about to give his son any ideas.

Maybe she should have insisted on helping in the kitchen instead of allowing Angie to bustle her out when she offered to help. Initially, Eve had been relieved not to have to chit-chat with Brenda, but she was beginning to wonder if she'd jumped out of the proverbial frying pan into something much worse than fire. This was hell.

From the quirk of his mouth as Chad poured drinks, Eve knew he sensed her dilemma. She grimaced. He wouldn't be looking so smug if the situation were reversed and it was his girlfriend—whoever she was— sitting here in his living room with his wife in the kitchen. Eve might just point that out to him when she had a chance.

"Are you feeling all right?" Brian asked.

Her gaze flew to him. "I'm fine."

"You look a little distracted."

Distracted? Good grief. How was she supposed to look, given the circumstances? "I was just thinking about, um, school."

"School?" Trey asked.

"Ah…yes. I…can't remember if I locked up all the supplies."

His mouth smiled, but his eyes didn't. "You don't leave stuff around."

Eve forced her own smile. She didn't lie well, and she suspected Trey knew it. "Well, you're probably right. Everything is put up."

"Speaking of put up," Chad said as a giggling Jessica burst into the room from the kitchen, pursued closely by Angie, "I thought we were supposed to have a sitter."

"She backed out this morning," Angie said, dabbing at gravy on her shirt. "Come on, Jessie. Mommy needs you in the kitchen."

"I suspect a child is the last thing you need in the kitchen right now," Eve said, glad that a diversion had been created. "Let her stay. She can sit with me."

"Oh, thank you!" Angie turned and hurried back through the door.

Three pairs of male eyes turned to Eve. Chad looked so shocked, his mouth had actually dropped open. Brian raised both brows, and Trey looked almost amused. Why?

Did they all think she couldn't handle a small child?

How hard could it be? Eve held out her hand. "Come sit with me, Jessica,"

Jessica stared at her from the middle of the room and didn't move.

"It's all right. Come here."

She shook her head vigorously. "No."

Chad frowned. "*Jessica.* Do as you're told."

Her lower lip trembled, and she began to cry.

God in heaven. Eve stared at the child. Why was she crying?

The sound turned into a loud wail as nobody moved.

The kitchen door swung open again and Brenda came out, a plate of appetizers in one hand. Setting them on the coffee table, she held out her hand to the child. "Come on, sweetie."

Jessica's tears dissolved into a bright smile like a rainbow after a shower. She clasped Brenda's hand happily and skipped alongside her to the kitchen.

"That's my mom," Trey said with more than a hint of pride.

Eve felt heat rush to her face and she looked down. A toddler had managed to defy her. Worse, the wife of her lover had swept in and handled the situation with ease. Could Eve be any more embarrassed?

"Don't let it bother you," Brian said. "Brenda has always been good with kids."

Her face felt as though it were going up in flames. Brian had noticed. Her mortification was complete. Damn it. She could handle high school kids. Eve raised her head, only to find Trey studying his father before he turned his gaze back to her.

"Why should it bother you?" Trey asked.

"Don't ever ask a woman 'why' unless you have a

couple of hours," Chad intervened, with a laugh as he picked up the plate of appetizers. "Let's start on these. They look good."

"They are," Trey said. "My mom made them. She's a great cook."

Of course she was. Brenda was one of those women who was perfect at everything. She always looked like she had just come from a photo shoot, yet she could handle holiday dinners and crying kids at the same time, not to mention running huge charity benefits. Eve had no doubt Brenda's house was immaculate, too. Maybe the woman should run for president of the United States.

Brian cleared his throat, and Eve glanced over at him. His dark eyes smoldered with an intensity she recognized. Desire pulsed through her instantly, her nipples pebbling as he lifted a corner of his mouth in unspoken invitation.

Eve inclined her head slightly in acceptance. *Later*.

Maybe there was one area in which Brenda hadn't achieved perfection after all.

Chapter Fifteen

Eve rolled on her side and traced Brian's collarbone with her fingertip as she held up the sex beads they'd just used with her other hand. . "This is a rather unique gift."

"You're a pretty unique person."

She studied him. "Do you mean that?"

"Sure. How many women would—" Brian stopped abruptly and raised up on an elbow. "Are you still thinking about yesterday's fiasco?"

"I wouldn't call the dinner a fiasco. The turkey was roasted to perfection," Eve said, deliberately not picking up his train of thought.

"That isn't what I meant."

"Let's not talk about it."

Brian hesitated and then he lay back, staring up at the ceiling. "Believe me when I say one of the things I truly appreciate about you is that you ask no questions, but I want you to know there's no reason to be jealous of Brenda."

"I'm not jealous." Eve flopped onto her back and stared at the ceiling too.

"Wrong word maybe. I just know how my wife affects most women. She's always taken care of herself because she's a perfectionist, ambitious, determined—"

"You really don't have to extol her virtues. I wasn't doubting them."

"Eve." Brian turned and took her hand. "What I'm

trying to say is that Brenda is her own woman. We've pretty much led separate lives for years."

"Hmmm. Then why do you stay?" God in heaven! Had she actually asked that? She, who prided herself on not interfering? "Forget I said that! I have no right to ask."

"It's okay. You and I have been together long enough." Brian released Eve's hand and propped himself against the headboard. "Trey. The kid has been getting into trouble ever since middle school. Brenda is too lenient with him."

Eve eased herself against the headboard too. "Not that he'd mention it at school, God forbid, but Trey does seem to be very proud of her."

"Yeah. She's always defended him." Brian shrugged. "I guess the kid knows which side of the bread has the butter on it."

Eve frowned. "Do you argue... Oh, my God. I'm doing it again. Asking too many questions."

"I don't get any warm fuzzies at home." Brian leaned toward her and nuzzled her neck while one hand slid to her breast and began to knead it. "Is that answer enough?"

"Ummm. Just keep on doing what you're doing and let me think about it," Eve answered as she slid lower and tugged Brian on top of her.

"Minx," he said.

****

"Everyone seems to have so much energy after vacation!" Molly exclaimed to Joni as some of the teachers milled around their mailboxes chattering.

Joni laughed. "That will probably last until the end of first period."

"Hey, I heard that," Eve said as she tossed half her mail into the trash. "The kids will be lethargic until at least lunchtime, so it should be an easy morning."

"True," Arthur Conrad said as he tossed most of his mail in the trash as well and turned to Joni and Molly. "How were your holidays, ladies?"

"I went to a buffet with friends," Joni said.

"And I went home," Molly replied.

"Where's home?"

"The Hill Country. A little town called Calle Verde."

"Small world," Arthur said. "I'm originally from Kerrville, but I didn't go back this year."

Molly wondered if it had anything to do with him losing his wife last year, but she didn't want to ask and stir memories. "The weather was pretty warm. I'm hoping there'll be snow for Christmas, though. Don't you love a white Christmas?" She clapped a hand over her mouth. How could she have been so stupid to say that? If anything, it would be a *blue* Christmas for him, and that didn't have anything to do with her mother's songs from the Elvis CD. 'I'm sorry. I didn't mean—"

"It's okay," Arthur said softly and then turned to Eve. "I wonder if Trey will be back today."

A frown passed over Eve's face. "His mother said he would."

"Oh. Did you talk to her before we left for the holiday? I didn't miss a conference, did I?"

"No and no. I went to a friend's place for Thanksgiving. He works for Trey's father, and the Caldwells were invited also."

"That's good. Did you get a chance to talk to Trey about the fight?"

Eve shook her head. "It wasn't the right time."

"I can see that. It probably would have spoiled the dinner for everyone. I would really like to work with him, though," Arthur said. "Encourage him to stay on the right track and out of trouble."

"Good luck. He's wandered off that track a couple of times already." Eve paused. "He seems to be friends with Ravati Singh, though, and she's a good kid."

Arthur brightened. "Yes, she is, and she's in the chess club. Maybe I can get Trey to participate in that. I'll talk to him later."

The tardy bell rang, and the teachers hurried off to their classes. Molly turned to Joni. "Gosh, I feel so bad for talking about wanting a white Christmas with family in front of Mr. Conrad."

"Don't worry. He went through counseling."

"He's just always so pleasant. I didn't mean to make him feel bad."

"He'll be okay."

"Still. I'd like to make it up to him." She thought for a moment and then opened her eyes wide. "I know! Gran gave me a bunch of small jars of jelly she sells in the craft shop, and some little loaves of nut breads, as well. I was going to make up a basket for Chad, but I can put together one for Arthur, too."

"Ummm, that sounds good," Joni said. "Can you make three?"

"Sure. I should have enough," Molly replied as Mrs. Wilson stomped on through, a frown on her face.

"On second thought, maybe you need to give some jelly to *her*," Joni said in a whisper. "It might sweeten that disposition."

Molly giggled. "Maybe I will."

****

"All right," Eve said as she finished taking roll and passed out an instruction sheet, "we've got three weeks before Christmas vacation—" She waited as half the students gave a rowdy cheer which woke up the half who looked like the walking dead. "And we've got a major project due as part of your final grade." A collective groan from the entire class, save for Trey, followed that remark.

Eve had wondered if he'd say something when he walked in, but he'd just gone to his seat. She was relieved he hadn't mentioned the dinner, since she didn't want her other students getting the idea that she socialized with any of them. She always made it clear at the beginning of the year that she wouldn't participate in Blog Facing any of them. If there was one thing teens valued in adults, it was fairness. Besides, there were too many reports in the news about educators getting into trouble using social media.

"Can we do our projects on our iPads?" one of the boys asked.

"No. I actually want you to be creative using your own imaginations."

"We can be creative using our tabs."

Eve shook her head. "You would be using the creativity of whoever designed the programs and apps. While I agree there is a commercial use for those, everything still begins with the neurons firing inside your heads."

Trey partially raised his hand. "What if we designed the program itself?"

"Designed the program?"

"Yeah." He glanced down at the paper she'd passed

out. "According to this, you want us to use perspective to draw what looks like a three-dimensional building. Wouldn't it be just as creative to design a computer program that would do that?"

"Hey, that would be cool!" another student said.

Ravati turned around in her seat, her eyes rounding. "Can you really do that?"

"Sure. No problem." Trey's dark gaze shifted back to Eve. "If she'll let me."

Eve paused. Trey was challenging her in a passive-aggressive way, like people who smilingly agreed with her and then did the opposite of what she expected. She couldn't deny that actually designing a drawing program would be creative—she wouldn't even know how to begin—but it wasn't the assignment. It didn't help that Ravati, the one person most of Trey's teachers felt would be a good influence, was impressed with the idea. And, given what Eve had seen of the relationship Brenda had with her son, his mother would probably be at the school tomorrow wanting answers, if Eve said no. She took a deep breath. Handling subtle aggression was a lot harder than dealing with outbursts and insubordination.

"I agree that designing a program would be a creative challenge." Eve looked around the room. "If several of you want to work on such a project, I will be glad to consider extra credit and also share your work with Mr. Thatcher, if you're in his class. However, the syllabus for this class remains pen-and-ink renderings, done individually." She picked up her sheet before anyone could argue. "Now, if you'll look at your instructions, we are going to be putting together a small city with various buildings dating from the 1800s." Eve picked up a small, open box from her desk. "I have buildings designated on slips of paper. Each of you will take one from the box. If you don't like yours, you're welcome to trade with someone else. Ravati, would you pass the box around, please?"

Trey's eyes narrowed so slightly Eve wouldn't have noticed except she was watching for his reaction. He wouldn't refuse to take a slip from the box with Ravati passing them out, but Eve was pretty sure she'd be hearing from Brenda.

Eve sighed. Things with Brian kept getting better and better. His latest sex toy Saturday had been truly amazing, sending her to multiple orgasms each time, yet it seemed the steamier things became with her lover, the more involved his family was becoming in their relationship as well.

So not good.

****

Molly had just finished assembling her jelly baskets late Monday afternoon when her doorbell rang. Putting down the roll of ribbon, she went to the door and peeked out the peephole. A huge arrangement of flowers was all she could see.

"Oh, my goodness!' she said as she opened the door. "Are those for me?"

"If you're Molly Whitfield they are," said a disembodied voice from behind the greenery.

"Yes! Yes, that's me! How exciting!"

The delivery boy lowered the vase enough so he could peer over it. "Where would you like me to put it?"

"On the table. Come in," Molly said and hurried to move the baskets and ribbon to the counter. "Right there will be fine."

After she'd tipped him and he left, Molly stared at

the cluster of two dozen red anthuriums, several sprigs of ginger, and a scattering of wood roses, all topped with a magnificent bird-of-paradise bloom. How very Hawaiian!

Molly reached for the small envelope and pulled out the card. Chad! The flowers were from Chad! He must have remembered her talking about the cruise. He'd written, "A symbolic token of my feelings, luv."

She hugged herself and twirled around her tiny kitchen before grabbing her phone and logging on to Blog-Face.

—I just received your *luv*-ly flowers! They're beautiful. Thank you!!!—

A moment later, the reply came.

—Do you see the symbolism?—

—Not sure what you mean.—

—Take a close look at the anthuriums. Use your imagination.—

Molly took a closer look. The flowers were shaped like hearts with a long, yellow stamen protruding out. She furrowed her brows. Hearts were symbols of love, but the thick shaft? Her cheeks suddenly heated as she realized the word she'd used and remembered some kid in her high school biology class snickering over the flower looking like a phallic symbol. Oh, my! Could Chad mean that?

—Ummm. I think I'm having naughty thoughts.—

—I hope so. I'm saving the best for last.—

—Best for last?—

—I also ordered a plumeria lei. I'll bring it over tomorrow night.—

—Can you come over tonight?—

—Not tonight, luv.—

—I can't wait to see you.—

— (Laugh) Good to know. Think about that lay.—

—I will.—

It was only after Molly had disconnected that she realized he'd misspelled the word. Her cheeks warmed again.

Or had he?

Chapter Sixteen

All day Tuesday, Chad found himself looking forward to seeing Molly later. Time seemed to drag, the tedious expense reports taking even longer than usual. Video of several potential recruits wasn't working and his varsity defensive team fumbled more of their drills than the freshman squad did. The day just didn't seem to end.

Chad couldn't remember the last time he had wanted sex as much as he did with Molly. Realizing she was a virgin—and it would be his "first time" with one of those—was absurdly exciting. Anticipating being a woman's initial experience and making sure the act was so well executed that no other man would ever compare to him was a compelling challenge he couldn't turn down. Fantasizing about how tight Molly would be made his member swell to proportions he hadn't realized since his college days.

What surprised Chad, though, was how playing the gallant knight titillated him. Meeting for drinks, going to a movie, holding hands, chaste kisses… Hell, he hadn't even done that in high school. This business of going slowly was an incredible high. Not only did setting self-imposed limits build sexual tension to near torture, but he actually found himself enjoying the prolonged agony, suspecting the end result would truly be the proverbial ecstasy. And that, in his somewhat jaded world, would be worth the wait.

Molly's open, undeniable pleasure in his efforts was something else he hadn't experienced. The women he'd dated when he was single expected to be taken to expensive places. Even the ones he just took to bed now still wanted money spent on them. Molly was content with that tucked-out-of-the-way retro pub and a simple indie movie, which was probably why he'd decided to send her the Hawaiian flowers. The only time Chad had ever sent flowers to any woman was Angie, after they became engaged—and that was because his grandmother had told him to.

The choice of anthuriums had been a stroke of luck, although it probably didn't seem so to the gay florist who'd suggested them when Chad had asked for something unusual. The man had mentioned their erotic symbolism and then held Chad's gaze a bit too long before his eyes had travelled over the rest of Chad's body in open suggestion. He'd pretended not to notice, but made clear the flowers were going to a girlfriend.

Chad glanced at the wall clock. Almost five o'clock. Molly would be home by now. He went to the small fridge he kept in his office and took out the plumeria lei. Not that he had any intention of having full-blown sex this afternoon—he didn't want to hurry it, strangely enough—but he did want to tease Molly a bit about the term, to gauge her reaction. It would give him an indication what path he needed to take. If she were truly as naïve as she seemed, the consummation of his endeavors would be like plucking an expensive pearl out of an oyster.

His cell dinged as he was about to leave. Chad glanced down at the text from Angie. "Call me immediately."

Crap. He'd told her he'd be working late. What could she want? With a sigh, he hit the connect button.

Angie answered on the first ring. "Thank God you had your phone close."

He tried to keep the annoyance out of his voice. "What did you want?"

"It's Jessica." Angie began to sob hysterically. "She fell and hit her head. We're in the ER at Parkland. How fast can you get here?"

Holy crap. His first inclination was to ask for details, but when Angie worked herself into an emotional frenzy, he wouldn't get any sense out of her. "On my way."

Disconnecting the conversation, Chad tapped on Blog-Face.

—Sorry, luv. Have to cancel. Family emergency. I'll explain when I can.—

Logging off without waiting for a reply, Chad returned the lei to the fridge. There was always tomorrow.

****

"Why so glum?" Joni asked Molly the next morning as she set her coffee mug on the desk next to the phone.

"I'm worried about Chad."

"Why? From the picture you took of those flowers, I'd say you don't have anything to worry about. If a guy is going to spend that kind of money, he's into you."

"It's not that." Molly looked down the corridor to make sure Mrs. Wilson was on her way in the other direction. "He was supposed to be in town yesterday, but he sent me a message that there had been a family emergency."

Joni's eyebrows lifted. "What kind of emergency?"

"I don't know. When I messaged back, I didn't get an answer. That's why I'm worried. He could have been in a car accident or something."

"Doubtful," Joni said and patted her hand. "Think about it, Molly. If Chad's hurt, he'd hardly be able to Blog-Face, would he?"

"I hadn't thought about that."

"Okay, so how much of a family does he have?"

"I'm not sure. I know he's divorced, but he never mentions his ex. He's never mentioned any brothers or sisters either. He told me his grandmother raised him. Oh!" Molly stopped as a distressing thought occurred. "Maybe something happened to his grandma! I don't know how old she is, but maybe she fell and broke a bone—"

"Stop imagining the worst," Joni said. "Why don't you just Blog-Face him again and ask?"

"But he didn't answer my last one."

Joni rolled her eyes. "You must have really grown up in Mayberry. Women don't have to wait to be called anymore." She smiled to soften her words. "This is the twenty-first century, not the fifteenth. Chivalry died a long time ago."

"That's not true. Chad has wonderful manners—"

"Excuse me," said Arthur Conrad as he approached and set a poinsettia plant on the counter between their desks. "I don't mean to interrupt, but I just wanted to say 'thank you' for the great basket of goodies you left for me yesterday."

"You're very welcome," Molly replied. "I felt really bad about bringing up sad memories for you."

A shadow flitted across his face, and then he smiled. "Don't feel bad. I'm learning to live with the loss.

Anyway, I had some of your grandmother's jelly on my toast this morning. It was delicious."

"I'll tell her you liked it."

"Please do," he answered and turned to leave. "Have a good day."

Molly watched him disappear around the corner and then reached out to touch a velvety red leaf on the plant. "You see, Joni, Mr. Conrad is a gentleman. Maybe chivalry isn't dead."

"Okay, I'll admit Mr. Conrad is a throwback to the Nice Guys Club, although I don't think it has very many members."

"Chad is—"

"Oh, for heaven's sake! Just go ahead and Blog-Face the guy," Joni said.

Molly fidgeted, finally reaching into her purse and then hesitated. "Mrs. Wilson isn't coming down the hall, is she?"

Joni shook her head. "I saw Mrs. Caldwell go in there a little while ago. I suspect they're having a conference."

"All right, then." Molly took out her phone and logged on.

—I don't mean to pry, but is everything all right?—

Nervously, she laid the phone in her lap, worrying her lower lip when a message didn't pop back up.

"Give it time, sweetie," Joni said, glancing down the hall, "and look busy. Mrs. Caldwell just left the office."

Molly grabbed a stack of papers and started sorting them.

"You've got them upside down."

"Oh." Molly felt her face warm as she righted them. She had no idea what they were and gave herself a mental shake. She'd never slacked off on a job before. Joni was right. She shouldn't worry. She needed to concentrate on what she was getting paid to do.

The papers were flyers for the teachers' mailboxes, advertising a discount at a local educational store. Slipping her phone into a drawer, Molly distributed them and returned to her desk. From now on, she would focus on work.

Her cell pinged. Leftover flyers fluttered to the floor as Molly pulled the drawer open in haste, hitting the "on" button with trembling fingers. Chad!

—Sorry, luv. Been a tough night. My grandmother fell, bumped her head.—

—Is she all right?—

—She will be fine. Just has to stay in hospital a couple of days.—

—I'm glad to hear she's not badly hurt.—

—Thanks, luv. See you soon.—

—Soon then.—

"It was his grandmother," Molly said as she logged off. "She did fall, but thankfully she didn't break anything."

"There. You see, you were worrying about nothing."

"I suppose," Molly said as she put her phone away—just in time, since Mrs. Wilson was rounding the corner. Even the principal's permanently dour look couldn't dampen her elation that everything was all right with Chad.

She might even have enough jellies and breads left to make a basket for Chad to take back to Waco. His grandmother would probably like that.

****

Eve wasn't surprised when Mrs. Wilson's secretary

buzzed her room and let her know Mrs. Caldwell was there and requesting Eve to meet with her. "Request" was simply a euphemism the secretary used because she tried to stay neutral. "Edict" would be more appropriate.

But then, Eve had expected Brenda to show up since Trey's project had been turned down. Deer Hill High School had more than its share of hovering helicopter-parents, and Eve had already seen how protective Brenda could be. She pasted on a smile as she entered the office.

"They're in there," the secretary said, indicating the "war room." Eve nodded, knocked lightly, and turned the doorknob.

"Thank you for coming," Brenda said as Eve entered the room.

"Not a problem," Eve replied, taking the seat Mrs. Wilson pointed to. At least Brenda wasn't hostile like some of the parents were when their kids didn't get their way about something. "I assume you're here about Trey's proposed project?"

For a moment Brenda looked confused, and then she shook her head. "If you mean wanting to create a technology application instead of doing an actual drawing, no."

Eve tried to hide her surprise. "No?"

"No. Trey told us about it, arguing the point that we lived in the twenty-first century, but Brian told him teachers had the final say." Brenda paused, giving Eve a studious look. "I must say, I agree with my husband on this. Our son spends way too much time on the computer as it is. Art, after all, has the ability to touch one's soul."

"Or at least to spark a slight interest," Eve replied wryly.

"Yes, art has a purpose," Mrs. Wilson said, "but

Mrs. Caldwell is here because of the altercation that took place before Thanksgiving."

"Before... You mean the fight?" Eve asked. "I thought that had been resolved."

"So did I," Brenda answered, "but we received a letter from an attorney for the other student that his parents are suing us in civil court."

"For what?"

"It seems the other boy suffered a concussion when he fell and now claims to have blurry vision and headaches."

Eve turned to Mrs. Wilson. "Didn't he return to school?"

The principal picked up a paper from her desk. "According to the registrar, he withdrew to be home-schooled."

"That's convenient," Eve said.

"We thought so too," Brenda replied. "I'd like to ask for your help."

"Me?" Eve felt confused. "What can I do?"

"First of all, Trey said all this started when he bumped into the other student in front of your class. Is that correct?"

"Yes. Trey was texting and ran into him. The other kid called him a jerk and he answered the same way."

"So the other student actually made a derogatory remark first?"

"Yes. I put a stop to it as soon as I could."

Brenda smiled. "I'm sure you did. Since it seems we're going to court, I'd like to ask you to testify for us."

Damn it. Eve strove to keep her facial expression impassive. She did not want further involvement with Brian's family. She'd been forced to have way too much contact as it was. Whatever was happening to her neatly compartmentalized life? Lovers had a niche. Wives and kids did not. *Damn it*. But Brenda was waiting for an answer. "I'm not sure if school policy allows faculty to testify one way or the other."

Mrs. Wilson stared at her as though she'd grown snakes on her head like Medusa. "Of course you can. You don't want a subpoena, do you?"

God, she hadn't thought of that. Would Brian... No, the question was, would Brenda take it that far? Eve glanced unobtrusively at the other woman. Her expression was placid, but Eve suspected the look was cultivated over years of fundraising persuasion. Brenda probably understood hardball as well as Metro U's coaching staff.

Eve was no stranger to the concept either, having dealt with high school students for years. Sometimes it was better to accept fate graciously rather than admit defeat.

"Of course. I'll be glad to do what I can."

"Thank you!" Brenda gathered her bag and rose. "I'll let you know the details as soon as we find out."

Eve nodded as Mrs. Wilson showed Brenda out. Walking to her room a short time later, Eve had the sinking feeling she was getting mired down in one of her ancestors' treacherous Irish bogs.

****

"I hear practice didn't go so well today," Brian said to Chad as he came to the office to turn in expense reports Wednesday afternoon. The guy looked tired.

"Yeah, defense was really clumsy today. Too much turkey, I guess. I'll hound them tomorrow," Chad answered as he slid into the seat in front of Brian's desk.

"I had a pretty rough night myself."

Brian turned up a corner of his mouth in a quirk. "Girlfriends sometimes have that effect. Too much sex?"

Chad grinned. "Is that possible?" Then he shook his head. "Nah. I didn't get any last night. Angie called just as I was getting ready to go. Jessica hit her head and ended up in the ER."

"Is it serious?"

. "I don't think so. Doc said there wasn't any sign of a concussion, but they wanted to keep her for observation for a couple of days."

"Good news, then."

"Yeah, except Angie was nearly hysterical. I spent most of the night trying to get her to calm down."

Brian nodded. "Mothers are like that. I remember a couple of times my older son landed in the ER due to sports injuries. Brenda threatened to make him stop playing football once."

"Bet that didn't go over well."

"Nope. Especially since I was still coaching high school at the time."

"At least you don't have that problem with Trey."

"Trey's a whole different ball game. The kid is smart, but he just doesn't put it to good use—unless you call being glued to the computer good use."

"Well, technology is a wide-open field. Maybe he'll be the next Steve Jobs."

"Doubtful. He can't seem to stay out of trouble."

"What's he done now?"

Brian shrugged. "Remember that skirmish he got into before Thanksgiving?"

"Yeah. Eve said he got suspended. Did he get into another scrap?"

"No, thank God, but the parents of the other kid want to take us to court."

Chad stared at him. "You're kidding. For exchanging a few blows? What kind of a wimp is the other kid anyway?"

"Don't know. According to the lawyer, the kid says he's having side effects."

"Jesus. What are attorneys going to do next? Haunt elementary playgrounds?"

"Don't give anyone any ideas." Brian took a deep breath. "The worst part is Brenda went to school today to ask Eve to testify."

"Holy crap. That will appeal to Eve about as much as jumping into shark-infested waters." Chad paused a minute. "Actually, I guess you could say she *is* jumping into shark-infested waters."

"And we're not referring to lawyers." Brian sighed. "When Eve agreed to be my mistress, she asked me to keep my family separate. She didn't want to get involved with my wife or kids and I didn't want her to. If Trey hadn't transferred to Deer Hill, none of this would be happening."

"Well, Eve's smart," Chad said as he got up to leave. "You can count on her being discreet."

"I know. It's one of her traits I really appreciate."

Chad grinned. "I'll bet there are other traits as well."

Brian grinned back. "Get out of here."

"Just saying," Chad responded and left before Brian could reply.

After he left, Brian picked up the expense reports, giving them a cursory look before signing off. He noticed the florist bill for Chad's girlfriend was on one page, although the explanation was holiday decoration for work-related dinner. A little fudgy, but it would probably pass scrutiny.

Brian laid the reports down. Did Eve like flowers? He didn't know. She'd never indicated she expected any kind of gift. She didn't even hint at going places with him either. She always seemed satisfied with the take-out dinners he took over. What she did want was sex—and lots of it. A man couldn't ask for a better mistress.

Perhaps he hadn't really appreciated Eve enough. He sure as hell didn't want to lose her over the current events. Brian looked at the expense reports again. The florist shop's number was included, and he reached for his phone.

Maybe he needed to practice a little old-time courting of his own. It certainly couldn't hurt.

Chapter Seventeen

Brenda pushed her Danish aside Thursday morning, sipped her coffee, and looked down at the notification of the lawsuit she'd left lying on the dining room table. She'd put it there yesterday after she'd come home from Trey's school. So far, neither Brian nor her son had bothered to look at it.

It wasn't as though they didn't know about the lawsuit. When the certified letter arrived Monday, she'd called Brian at his office. He'd made a few choice remarks about how the whole thing wouldn't have happened if they'd sent Trey to that school outside Fort Worth. Brenda had decided to temporarily retreat rather than engage in battle. Brian generally left most of the guidance of their son to her, but he'd been adamant about that horrible boys' camp thing, and she didn't want to push the issue.

Trey was another matter. He'd just shrugged when he got home from school and said the other boy had started it.

Brenda heard him clomping down the stairs and cringed. Trey had a wiry build, so how could he possibly make so much noise? She listened as he made his way to the foyer. His backpack thumped to the floor. He was probably reaching for his coat.

"Please join me," she called out.

A momentary silence preceded his appearance in the

162

doorway. He leaned against the frame, one arm in his long black coat, dangling the backpack while the other hand reached behind him for the second sleeve. "What?"

Brenda gestured to a place setting of cereal, a small pitcher of cream, orange juice, and a buttered croissant. "Join me."

"I don't have time for breakfast."

"This morning you do."

Something in her tone, which she kept low and well-modulated, must have alerted him. Dropping the backpack, Trey shrugged out of his coat, letting it fall to the floor as well, and walked over to the table where he slouched down in the chair. "What do you want?"

"A civil tone, for one thing," she said and slid the letter toward him. "We need to talk about this."

He frowned and pulled off a piece of roll. "There's nothing to talk about."

"Oh, I think there is. Your father is quite upset over this."

Trey looked up. "Why should he care? He's never around."

"There's nothing I can do about that. You know running an athletic department is more than just an eight-to-five job."

"If you say so."

Brenda sighed. This problem had been on-going since Little League days. Brian had wanted to raise Trey like he had Tom, who thrived on competition and sports. When Trey had shown no indication—or particular skill—Brian had lost interest. Moving up the coaching ladder, first to high school head coach and then to the school district AD, had indeed consumed most of Brian's time. Trey had taken it as determined avoidance. When

Brian entered the collegiate world of sports and Trey drifted into the world of cyberspace, the conflict had only grown worse.

"Do you know how close your father is to sending you to one of those schools for delinquent youths?"

Trey's eyes darkened, and he put down the spoon he'd just picked up. "He wants to get rid of me that much?"

"He doesn't want to get rid of you, dear. In his own way, he loves you."

"Yeah, right."

Brenda sighed again. The same old argument. Brian was not a physically affectionate man, nor was he high on verbal praise, and Trey, as a child, had craved hugs and attention. He'd outgrown that urge—or at least repressed it—at about the age of nine. It had remained a contention of sorts, even though Brenda had no doubt Trey would deny any need for praise from his father as adamantly as Brian would the need to give it. "He wants what's best for you. Some of the decisions you've made lately haven't been that good. Your father is concerned."

"Yeah, right."

"I don't agree that this boys' school is where you need to go, but—"

"Thanks."

"You're welcome." Brenda wasn't sure if Trey meant it, but she'd at least pretend he did. "I managed to convince him to let you give Deer Hill a try. The thing is, there were problems at the old school, and now this fight at the new school."

Trey frowned again. "Dad is the one who always told me to defend myself."

"Defend yourself, yes. Instigate a fight, no."

"The other guy started it!" Trey's eyes darkened. "Don't you believe me?"

"I believe you. In fact, Ms. O'Connor backed up your story when I went to school yesterday."

He stared at her. "You did what?"

Brenda sensed a storm might be brewing, but she kept her voice calm. "I went to school to gather facts for our case. I've asked Ms. O'Connor to testify."

"Oh, Christ. That's just great."

"Don't swear, please." Brenda tapped the letter with a manicured fingertip. "This may not seem vital to you, but being sued is serious business. You have no idea of how much damage can be done."

Trey looked at the letter, then pushed his chair back and stood. "I gotta get to school. My first period is with Ms. O'Connor. It probably won't look good if I'm late."

His voice held more than a trace of sarcasm, but Brenda let it go. One had to choose one's battles wisely. She looked at the lawsuit notification again.

This was one she was not going to lose.

****

"I can't decide if I like it better when I tie you up or you do me," Brian told Eve late Thursday afternoon as she sat astride his belly after riding him hard.

"You always like it when I do you," Eve replied, angling her hips so she could feel his spent erection still inside her.

Brian grinned and motioned to the padded leather wrist cuffs she'd just removed from him. "I was talking about these."

Eve grinned back. "I wouldn't want you to think you could go all Dom on me."

He growled, sat up, and rolled her backward without

165

breaking contact. His body pinned hers to the bed. "No? How does this feel?"

She wiggled beneath him. "It feels like the big guy is ready to go again." Then she smiled slowly. "Show me."

It wasn't until sometime later, when their breathing had steadied and their heartbeats slowed, that Eve remembered the flowers Brian had sent. She rolled onto her side. "The roses were beautiful."

"I'm glad you liked them."

She propped her head on her hand. "What's the occasion?"

"No occasion. I just wanted to let you know I appreciate you."

Eve stroked his penis. "I've gotten that impression."

"That's not what I mean." He paused as her fingers continued to fondle him. "Or maybe it is. Anyway, since we don't go out—"

"I don't expect you to date me," Eve replied. "That wasn't part of the deal."

"Neither was getting involved with my family. Especially not this current mess."

"Ummm." Eve let her fingers linger a bit longer and then sat up, reaching for her robe. "It's not your fault."

Brian grimaced as he stood, slid on his jeans, and then picked up his shirt. "I wish I could keep you out of it. Why the hell Trey picked Deer Hill to attend, I don't know."

Eve furrowed her brow. Brian had mentioned something about that before. "Trey actually chose the school, and not Brenda?"

"Yeah. Brenda knew I fully intended to send him to that alternative school, so I guess when he asked to go to

Deer Hill, she figured that was one less argument she'd have to win. Damn it. Any school but yours. Now you're involved in a legal mess."

"Well, we can't do anything about that. I guess I was just the lucky—or unlucky—person who witnessed the beginning of the altercation in the hallway that day. I'll just not offer any opinions on the witness stand."

Brian finished buttoning his shirt. "My lawyer is trying to settle out of court. According to Trey, the fight actually happened in an empty classroom and there weren't any witnesses. If he's not lying, that makes it a pretty flimsy case."

"Raising kids is tough. I'm glad I don't have any."

"I'm glad you don't either, but for purely selfish reasons. I don't want to share my mistress. By the way, have you talked to Chad?"

"Not recently. Why? Is he having trouble with his on-line girlfriend?"

"I don't think so, although he doesn't say much about her, contrary to his usual willingness to divulge all. I was talking about his kid."

"Jessica?

"Yeah. She fell and hit her head the other night."

"My God! Is she okay?"

"Seems to be. Just thought he might have told you, since Angie went hysterical and Chad had to forego his date."

"You're right. He usually blogs me when something like that happens."

"Well, don't worry about it." Brian lifted Eve's chin and swept a kiss across her lips. "Don't worry about the court thing either. I think I have everything under control."

****

"Dinner was wonderful!" Molly said to Chad as they came back to her apartment Thursday evening. "I didn't even know a Hawaiian restaurant existed in Dallas. I've only had mahi-mahi once. The flowers on the tables matched the ones you sent." She fingered her lei. "And this smells so good!"

"So do you," Chad replied and drew her into his arms as soon as she closed the door. "And I'll bet you taste even better." He covered her mouth with his, not giving her time to reply. Her lips were sweet, and it wasn't just the lingering scent of the pineapple they'd had for dessert. It was the way her soft curves fit perfectly against the straight planes of his body. It was the way she twined her arms around his neck, her fingers lightly plying his hair. It was the way she gave a breathy little sigh and parted her lips in open, innocent invitation.

An invitation he didn't hesitate to take advantage of. He touched the tip of his tongue to hers, teasing her, withdrawing a bit, only to have her fingers tighten instinctively on his neck, holding him in place. Chad drew Molly closer, deepening the kiss. She gave another small moan, tentatively returning his tongue's caresses. The sound and sensation were a heady combination, causing Chad's head to spin. He crushed Molly to him, his arms wound tightly around her, his mouth totally plundering hers. Never had he felt such a strong reaction to a woman. Heat soared through him. Not only did his manhood throb with aching need, but every other nerve ending was alive as well. He felt dizzy, as though he were floating in air and Molly was flying with him. It was as though they were melding into one being.

From some distance, the faint niggling of his logic

tried to intrude, warning him this was emotional involvement—that this woman would touch those inner feelings he kept carefully locked away. If he proceeded, she'd break down his barriers.

He pushed the thought away, half-carrying, half-dancing Molly toward the couch. He might have to pay the devil his due tomorrow, but tonight he would experience heaven. Molly was intoxicating. Maybe those religions that touted a warrior's reward was virgins in nirvana had something going for them. The combination of Molly's naïve innocence and her willing compliance was as addicting as any drug. He had to have her.

Easing her down on the sofa, he started to undo the buttons to her blouse, fingers aching to free her lush, full breasts.

"My flowers! They're all crumpled!"

Chad tore at the string holding the lei together and tossed it aside. "I'll buy you another one tomorrow, luv." He nearly fumbled in his haste to remove her shirt—something he'd always been adept at—and lifted her slightly to unhook the rather plain bra she wore.

Molly raised on her elbows. "What are you doing?"

"Shhh, luv. Just relax," Chad said soothingly as he lifted one of her arms to tug the garments off and then raised the other to totally eliminate the unnecessary clothes. "I'm just going to continue what I started last time."

"But…I shouldn't…*Ah!*"

The last sound came as Chad took her beaded nipple into his mouth and suckled. Pure male pride washed over him as she repeated the sound, her head now thrown back against the couch pillow. He moved to her other breast, drawing deep this time, his hand kneading the one he'd just left, his fingers tugging at the swollen nipple. Molly mewled, sighed, and whimpered, her back arching.

Before she could grab his head, though, he eased himself lower, keeping one hand plying her plump mounds while his other hand deftly made short work of pushing her skirt up and her panties down. No more fumbling now. The scent of her arousal hit him like a double shot of tequila.

Molly's eyes popped open and she attempted to push her skirt back in place. Chad caught her hands. "Just relax, luv. You're going to like this. I promise."

"But I shouldn't...we shouldn't...*Ah!*" she said again as he slid a finger into her sleek wetness. "Shouldn't...should—"

"Definitely *should*," Chad murmured, continuing to play with the pulsating little bud. "Does it feel good?"

"Er...yes. Yes. It feels fantastic."

Chad grinned. "Then you'll really like this." Before she could protest, he pushed her knees apart and slipped two fingers inside her. As she writhed, Chad began to have doubts he could wait for her to come before he took her completely. He teased a nipple and Molly gasped as her body trembled.

She trilled even as her muscles relaxed against his fingers, and Chad realized it was his phone that was ringing. He glanced at where he had laid it on the coffee table. Angie. Damn it. Not *now*.

The ringing finally stopped. His text pinged.

Molly struggled to a semi-sitting position, looking dazed and decidedly satiated. Just like he wanted a woman to be.

"Aren't you going to get that?"

"Not now. We're not through, luv."

Her eyes grew round. "We're not...oh!" Her face flushed a becoming shade of crimson. "Well, maybe we should move to the bedroom."

"An excellent idea."

His phone rang again. Angie.

Molly frowned. "Maybe it's important."

Probably not, but hell. If his wife was going to keep calling while he was in the middle of showing a virgin all the pleasures of sex, maybe he should get the call out of the way. "Hello?"

Hysterical crying greeted him. He put his hand to the phone, although he was pretty sure Molly couldn't hear it. "What's wrong?"

"Jessica!" Angie's voice rose shrilly. "She started running a high temp. I'm at the ER. Get here as fast as you can."

Chad drew a steadying breath, trying to ignore the still painful bulge in his pants. "All right. I'm on my way."

"What's wrong?" Molly asked when he disconnected.

"Ah...that was the nursing home in Waco. My grandmother's fallen again and they want me to get there as quickly as I can."

"Of course you must." Molly straightened her skirt and reached for her blouse. "If anything happened to my gran... Well, I can't imagine how horrible that drive will be." She followed Chad to the door. "Please drive carefully." She rose on tiptoe to kiss him. "Let me know how everything is?"

"Will do." He ended the kiss before his wayward body caused him to linger and hurriedly let himself out the door.

The crisp December air cooled his ardor somewhat. Oddly enough, the torture of stopping when he was about ready to explode was strangely arousing in itself. Maybe giving Molly time to contemplate and anticipate what would happen next would only increase her pleasure and his. After all, taking her virginity shouldn't be hurried. He would definitely look forward to that moment.

Meanwhile, he had to quiet his wife's hysterics.

****

"Thank God you're here!" Angie dried her tears as Chad entered the waiting area of the ER. "I'm about to lose it."

"Calm down." Chad looked around the room and led Angie to a corner. "Have you talked to any of the doctors yet?"

"Not yet. It's been nearly an hour." Her voice started to crack. "Maybe something's gone horribly wrong—"

"Stop it. First of all, if something were really wrong, they'd send a nurse or someone out here. Secondly, this is *Parkland* ER. Every major trauma gets sent here." He frowned. "Why didn't you call the pediatrician?"

"I did. I got voice mail that she's at a conference."

"She didn't leave a contact number for another doctor?"

"Yes, but it was after five." Angie looked around the crowded room. "I didn't know what else to do."

"Well, we're here. All we can do is wait."

Angie furrowed her brows. "Where were you? I called your office. The secretary said you'd left before four."

Chad shrugged. "Just stopped off for a drink."

"You can drink at home, you know."

"Heck, it was a tough day. I just wanted a little peace

and quiet." He changed the subject abruptly. "When did Jessica start running a fever? She was fine this morning."

"Not really. She started coughing yesterday. I got up twice during the night to get her some water."

"I didn't hear you."

"I tried to be quiet and didn't turn on a light. Anyway, the cough got worse and her little face turned really red this afternoon. That's when I took her temperature." She started to wring her hands. "I wish my mother was here."

One of Chad's eyebrows rose. "Your mother? What could she do? Does she have a magic wand or something?"

The idea of her mother waving a wand a la *Harry Potter* almost made Angie smile. "Don't be silly. She's just Mom. My baby is sick and I'm worried. I've not raised a child. I could use some advice and…and comforting. It's what moms do."

A shadow crossed Chad's face, and too late, Angie remembered his childhood. "I'm sorry. I didn't mean—"

"It's all right."

"What I meant was—"

"I know what you meant. Just drop it, okay?" He picked up a magazine and sat down. "Go ahead and call her if it makes you feel better."

She didn't want to tell Chad she already had while she was waiting for him to get to the hospital. The whole reason the remark had spilled out of her mouth was because her mother had offered to come up and Angie had told her it wasn't necessary. She'd only been having second thoughts because of the long wait.

Before she could think of what to say to Chad, the

double doors near them swung open, and a doctor in scrubs walked out. "Mrs. Olson?"

"Yes, right here." Angie hurried over to him as Chad followed. "How is Jessica?"

"It appears to be a case of pertussis—whooping cough," the doctor said. "Was she not vaccinated?"

"I…I don't think so."

"Does your daughter not have a pediatrician?"

"Yes, she does, but I… Well, Jessica hasn't been sick, so I didn't make any appointments." Angie looked at Chad and then back to the doctor. "I've been so busy this fall. I guess I forgot about the vaccinations."

"The doctor took a deep breath, reminding Angie that was the same thing Chad did when he was annoyed with her but didn't want to get into an argument. It was just that she'd been concentrating so hard on cooking and trying to be a homemaker…and she'd forgotten about her child's shots. How could she have done that? She deserved the doctor's ire.

"Once Jessica recovers, I'd suggest you make an appointment with her doctor and review her records."

"Oh, I will! I will. Can we take Jessica home now?"

The doctor shook his head. "I'd like to keep her in the hospital a few days. Pertussis can take its toll on small children, and Jessica was admitted just a few days ago for head trauma. I don't want to take any chances."

"That sounds like a good idea," Chad said.

The doctor looked from one of them to the other and nodded. Angie wasn't sure if he had decided to admit Jessica because of the whooping cough or because he thought they weren't capable parents for forgetting the shots. She felt tears welling up again. Maybe she should ask her mother to come up after all.

"You can see her before you leave."

"Yes, please," Angie said.

"Just one more thing," the doctor said as he led them through the doors past triage. "You're both carriers right now, so avoid close contact with your co-workers and neighbors for at least a week."

"I can do that," Angie replied and glanced at Chad who looked distracted. She turned to the doctor. "My husband is a football coach. Can he still work with his team?"

A corner of the doctor's mouth turned up. "As long as he doesn't tackle anyone."

Angie smiled with relief. At least Chad wouldn't have to miss any games. She looked at Chad, sure he'd be glad to hear that, but he was already texting a message as he followed them down the hall.

Probably to Brian, letting him know.

****

"Do you have plans for Christmas?" Arthur Conrad asked Joni and Molly on Friday morning. "We've just got one week left until break."

"That is, if we survive the kids," Eve said as she passed by the counter on her way to class. "The last week before Christmas always reminds me what it must have been like when Old West cowboys tried to drive a herd of wild cattle up the Chisholm Trail."

Arthur smiled. "An apt description, although I think the reenactment today's cowboys do through Fort Worth's stockyards is less problematic."

Molly giggled. "I've seen that. Daddy brought me up here one year when I was going through my horse-crazy stage, to watch."

"It's a good event," Arthur replied. "So, are you

175

going home?"

"Yes. I was going to leave Saturday, but I think I'll wait for Sunday."

Joni winked. "She's hoping the boyfriend will be back by then."

Eve watched Molly blush, wondering again what it must be like to be so in love…with the idea of love, at least. "Did he have to go somewhere?"

"Yes. He was at my place yesterday and got a phone call that his grandmother had fallen—she's in an assisted living place in Waco—and he had to go down to check on her. Then later, Chad blogged me saying he'd have to stay for most of the week."

Eve stared at Molly. It couldn't be the same person. "Chad? Your friend's name is Chad?"

"Yes. Chad Jensen. Why?"

Eve breathed a sigh of relief, but it was short-lived. Chad wasn't above using an alias, as Eve well knew. "What does he do, if you don't mind my asking?"

"I don't mind. He's a national marketing executive and travels all over helping colleges recruit high school athletes."

"I see." Eve kept her voice passive as bells clanged and sirens screeched inside her head. It could just be a coincidence that this guy worked with college athletes. She shouldn't assume Chad had created an alternate personality, even though she knew he was capable of doing so. At any rate, she had no right to burst Molly's bubble—at least not until she'd talked to Chad. "That sounds interesting. Does he talk about the job?"

Molly shook her head. "Not really. Mostly he asks questions about me. When I told him Gran had instilled a love of the old British bands in me, Chad took me to the Pendulum in the West End. Then, when I mentioned I loved my trip to Hawaii, he sent me an arrangement of tropical flowers from the All Things Polynesian florist shop at the mall." Molly smiled and blushed again. "He is such a gentleman."

Maybe this guy was who he said he was. Sending flowers didn't sound like Chad. Still, Eve decided it would be good to check it out.

But it wasn't until she got home that she had time. The day may not have originated in hell, but it had ended there. Someone had phoned in a bomb threat during second period, forcing an evacuation to the football field, where the students huddled together for over an hour in a cold north wind. Evidently, a number of them had seen fit to leave campus, against school rules, inciting Mrs. Wilson to get on the PA and insist on each teacher turning in an amended attendance report. To add fuel to the principal's already inflamed disposition, the halls had reeked of marijuana after lunch. Between having the Bomb Squad out in the morning and the Gang Unit with their K-Nines in the afternoon, Mrs. Wilson had clomped down every hall, glaring in classroom doors as though she could spot the culprits. Then the news media had returned *en masse*, bringing a fitful completion to a totally chaotic day.

And—God help them—they still had a week to go.

Eve tossed her bag onto the sofa and sank down beside it. Pulling out her phone, she brought up Chad's name.

—How about a drink? I could use one.—

—I could too, but I can't.—

—Oh? Date tonight with the girlfriend?—

Eve crossed her fingers, hoping it was so.

—Nope. Jessica at hospital again.—

—Oh, no! How serious is it?—

—Not serious. Whooping cough. Doc says we're carriers.—

—Carriers?—

—Yeah. Not supposed to make contact with others for a week.—

The bells started clanging in Eve's mind again. Red flags accompanied the sirens this time.

—That will put a damper on things.—

—Yeah. Gotta go. Later.—

Which meant Angie was nearby. Eve signed off and reached over to put her phone on the coffee table. As she did, her hand scraped the florist card beside the roses and it floated to the floor. Picking it up to put it back, she froze.

The roses had come from All Things Polynesian.

Chapter Eighteen

Four more days to go. Eve watched the last student leave her room Monday afternoon, tempted to bolt out right after the girl. But she still had to straighten up the room. She should just be grateful the kids were working on their projects and not bouncing off the walls.

The weekend had been crap. She was worried that Molly's boyfriend was really Chad Olsen, but Eve wanted to ask him that question face to face. He never had been good at lying to her. And if what she suspected was true, then he had to come clean with Molly. The girl might be in her early twenties, but she'd been sheltered by her family and her small town. She didn't deserve to be conned. Eve doubted that Molly would ever agree to an affair with a married man, but at least she should know how things stood.

Of course, maybe Eve was wrong. She wished she'd had a chance to talk to Brian, get his take on this. Maybe Chad had said something to him about who the girlfriend was. But Brian was in California at a national convention and wouldn't be back until tomorrow.

Eve had just shut off the lights when the intercom buzzed. Mrs. Wilson's secretary came on, asking that Eve come to the office. Crap. Being called to the office was becoming a nasty habit. Probably some residue from Friday's disaster. Just what she needed.

The secretary motioned that the principal was in her

office, not the war room. So this wasn't going to be something that involved other faculty. Eve put a pleasant expression on her face as she entered.

Mrs. Wilson sat at her desk, ramrod straight as an Army general. "Close the door and have a seat."

Eve complied. "Is one of my students in trouble?"

One steely gray brow rose. "I don't know. Perhaps."

Perhaps? Mrs. Wilson wasn't given to "maybe" and "perhaps." Eve had a sense of foreboding. "Why did you want to see me?"

Instead of answering, the principal opened a drawer and took out several sheets of paper. She slid them face down across the desk. "Several faculty members brought these in just a little while ago."

Frowning, Eve reached over to pick up the small stack. As she turned them over, she felt the blood drain from her head when she saw what it was.

Private blogs—the most recent one last Thursday afternoon—of conversations she'd had with Brian over the past weeks. Intimate conversations. Eve gulped air to combat her lightheadedness. This couldn't be happening. She'd used every security setting Blog-Face had. "How…why…?"

Mrs. Wilson's voice was grim. "I do not know how someone managed to obtain access to your account—Blog-Face is blocked on the school server—but someone did manage to copy them and hack into the school's email system to send this vile information to the faculty."

Another wave of dizziness hit Eve, and she gripped the chair arms. "The entire faculty got this?"

"Hopefully not. Mrs. Torres brought in the first copy just after the last bell rang. I contacted Mr. Hatcher to shut down the whole system immediately. We've got the

LAN manager working on deleting it. However—" Mrs. Wilson gestured to the papers "—some of the faculty did get those."

Dear God. "But why…who…" Eve's voice trailed off as both of Mrs. Wilson's eyebrows rose.

"I should think that would be obvious, although I don't know whether we can prove it."

A wave of nausea washed over Eve. The answer was more than obvious.

Trey.

****

"Oh, my God! Have you heard?" Joni rushed down the hall minutes later and around the counter to take her seat beside Molly. "Miss O'Connor's been hacked!"

"What do you mean, hacked?"

Joni dropped her voice to a whisper. "She's been having an affair with a married man!"

Molly widened her eyes in shock. "Miss O'Connor? How do you know that?"

"It's all over the school. Or at least it was until they shut down the server." Joni tapped the email icon on the front desk's computer, but it didn't open. "Too late."

"I don't think I understand."

"Well." Joni looked around conspiratorially before continuing. "She used her Blog-Face account to contact the man. Rumor has it the blogs were pretty risqué."

"That doesn't prove she was seeing him, does it?"

Joni rolled her eyes. "Why would she sext someone if she wasn't seeing him?"

Molly felt herself blush. It was hard to fathom someone would actually *talk* about doing…well, what Chad and she had done last week. Let alone going all the way. "Are you sure?"

Joni nodded. "One of the coaches said he'd always thought Miss O'Connor was hot, and if he'd known she was into married guys, he'd have hit on her himself."

"That's awful! Married men shouldn't think like that. They shouldn't even be flirting with other women."

"Good luck with that idea."

"I know it sounds naïve, but it's what I believe." Molly drew her brows together. "Maybe Miss O'Connor didn't know this man was married."

"Ha! The guy is the father of one of her students!"

"*What*? That can't be true."

"It's true, all right. He's Trey Caldwell's father."

"How do you know that?"

"The coach recognized his name. He's the Athletic Director at Metro U."

Molly deepened her frown. She remembered Mr. Caldwell attending one of the conferences. He was a very good-looking man. At the time, she'd thought Trey's parents looked so good together, his mother so blonde and elegant and his father so trim, with the dark hair and eyes like Trey's. "Miss O'Connor's met both of Trey's parents."

"So?"

"So she knows they're married."

"Duh."

"I don't understand why Miss O'Connor would get involved with him." Molly felt confused. "That's wrong."

"Cheating has been going on for millennia. Who knows why people do it?" Joni shut down the computer and picked up her purse to leave. "You can't change the world, sweetie."

"Maybe not." Molly gathered her things as well.

"But I would never do something like that. Ever."

****

"Vodka martini?" the bartender at Eve's favorite watering hole asked.

"Make it a double."

"Tough day?"

"You've no idea," Eve replied. "If you don't mind, would you bring the drink to that table in the back?"

"Sure thing," he answered. "You go sit."

She all but crumpled onto the chair. She'd spent last night in a daze, trying to make sense of everything. How her personal account could have been compromised, for starters. One of the reasons Blog-Face outpaced its rivals was because it offered tight security.

The bartender set her drink down. "Tab?"

"For sure." Eve took a big swallow and let the burning liquid slide down her throat. Setting the glass down before she could drain it, she bit into the olive.

Fortunately, all traces of the blogs had been deleted off the server by the time Eve got to school that morning. Eve suspected Mrs. Wilson had issued a non-negotiable order to the faculty and staff, because no one mentioned the horrendous incident. She'd received plenty of looks, though, ranging from shock and indignation to snarky and, in the case of a couple of male teachers, lecherous. Arthur Conrad and Irma Torres had exchanged pleasantries with her as though nothing was wrong, which had nearly broken down her resolve to keep her chin up and her eyes focused.

Worst, though, were the smirks from some of her students. They *knew*. Although they didn't have access to faculty computers, no doubt Trey had enjoyed passing copies of the blogs around yesterday, although he'd been conspicuously absent today. If she'd had any doubts Trey was behind all this, they were anything but alleviated when Ravati Singh came to her room after school.

Poor kid. She'd been trembling and crying, hardly able to get the words out. Eve finally managed to calm her down enough for the story to be told. Evidently, the Tech Club members had been competing with each other on building websites. Ravati had been having trouble with hers, and Trey had moved over to help, but only made it worse. He'd asked Mr. Thatcher to go help her and then sat down in the teacher's chair. It wasn't until Trey had bragged to Ravati about sending the blogs over the teachers' network that she realized he had set the whole thing up to gain access to Mr. Thatcher's computer. And then she'd started wailing again.

Eve took another—smaller—sip and watched as Brian appeared in the doorway. He paused, eyes adjusting to the light, and then rushed to the table. He slipped into a chair. "What's the matter? My secretary said it was urgent. Why didn't you blog?"

Eve waited for the bartender to take his order for Scotch. "You don't know?"

"Know what?" Brian looked around the bar. "Why are we meeting here instead of your place?"

"I thought it might be wise not to set ourselves up."

He looked confused as his drink was brought, but he waited for the bartender to leave before he spoke. "Set ourselves up for what?"

"To be caught by your wife."

Brian reached for his drink. "What has happened?"

Eve slid the sheaf of papers toward him and watched his face pale. When she finished explaining, he drained his glass.

"Christ. I knew that kid was up to no good." Brian motioned for a second round. "Why in hell would he do this?"

"He must blame me for the affair," Eve said, "but I don't know how he found out. I don't think we gave anything away at the Thanksgiving dinner, and we've always been discreet. How could he know?"

"I don't... God damn it!" .

"Sir?" The bartender set their drinks down. "Is everything okay?"

"Yes. Sorry."

"What is it?" Eve asked as Brian tossed the contents of his Scotch down.

"I just remembered something. I didn't think... Oh, hell." Brian shook his head. "This is all my fault."

Eve arched an eyebrow. "Your fault? It takes two to trip the tango."

"I don't mean us." Brian ran a hand through his hair. "The weekend that Trey got picked up for marijuana, I was about to blog you from the police station when we were called in. I stuffed the phone back into my briefcase, but I must have left the blog open. I just remembered it was Trey who picked the case up and followed us out. He must have seen the screen."

Eve frowned. "Even if he did, he'd only have seen my first name."

Brian shook his head again. "In the argument that ensued going home, I completely forgot about the phone. It wasn't until the next morning that I checked it. Trey would have had plenty of time to take it, backtrack through the blogs, check identities, obtain passwords, and return the phone."

"Good Lord." Eve felt the blood drain from her face for the second time in as many days. "That means…he knew about us before he even got to Deer Hill."

Brian grimaced. "Which is probably *why* he wanted to go to Deer Hill."

"So that's why he always watched me so intently. I felt like some strange organism under a microscope."

"He's a clever kid, I'll give him that much. He'd study you to find your weak spot, where you would be most vulnerable, and then he'd strike."

"He's done this before?"

"Kind of. Back when I was coaching high school, he accused me of flirting with the cheerleaders to get me into trouble because he didn't want to play football. Another time, he got caught with beer and insinuated that I had bought it for him. Luckily, the principal and I had gone to college together and he knew better, on both counts." Brian's eyes widened suddenly. "You're not going to lose your job, are you?"

"Doubtful. I didn't break any school policy. I didn't use the school computers. Nothing occurred on school property or at a school function. There was no involvement with students or faculty, for that matter." Eve smiled a little. "Believe me, no one in Central Administration is going to stack up a pile of rocks to throw at me. Too many of them live behind glass walls themselves."

"That's good to know, but you're still facing scandal."

"I'll admit it's been a rough two days, but the holidays are almost here. Life will be better when I get back."

"That's one of the things I respect you for. You take

it on the chin."

"Well, I knew there would be risks when we started this." Eve swirled the last contents of her martini before finishing it. "Speaking of risks, what about Brenda? How did she handle it?"

"She doesn't know."

"*What*? How can she not know?"

"Think about it. Trey planned this whole thing to ruin your reputation, not his mother's. He's always been protective of her."

"I saw that at Thanksgiving. He wasn't in school today, though, so I thought she'd kept him home."

"He told her he thought he was coming down with the flu. That's all it took." Brian sighed. "She's always been overly protective of him too."

"So they bond."

"Yes, much more so than our other son. Trey's always thought I played favorites, and maybe I did. I *understood* Tom."

"So you really don't think Brenda will find out?"

"Trey won't tell her. Our trysts are safe on that account. I'll change my password so he can't access any more blogs." Brian stood, took out his wallet, and tossed a couple of twenties on the table. "Why don't we go back to your place and let me make you feel all better? I do know what you like, babe."

Eve hesitated, and then she shook her head. "Much as I'd appreciate a good romp, I think I just want to be alone tonight."

His forehead creased, and then he bent over to kiss her temple. "Okay. Blog me when you're ready."

As Brian walked toward the door, Eve hesitated. She wanted the sex. Maybe she needed it. After the past two days of hell, she knew it would be intense. And she would feel so good after, so completely and totally exhausted and satiated. Eve started to rise and call out to him, and then she sank back.

Confusion reigned and she watched him leave.

Chapter Nineteen

Wednesday had been marginally better. Trey remained absent, and Eve suspected he wouldn't return for the rest of the week. Instead of enduring stares from the faculty, she found most of her colleagues went about their own business or were possibly just trying to keep their sanity until Winter Break started on Friday afternoon. Either way, Eve was grateful.

She shut off the lights in her classroom and closed the door. All she had to do was deliver some attendance papers to the front desk, and then she could go home. She had a lot of contemplating to do.

Molly was the only clerk working when Eve approached the counter. "These are the final reports from last Friday's incident," she said as she handed them over.

"Thanks, Miss O'Connor." Molly looked up and gave her a tentative smile. "I just wanted to say how sorry—"

The front door to the lobby swung open before she could finish. Someone wearing a hoodie and carrying a bundled toddler walked in. Eve blinked as the woman tossed back the hood. "Angie! What are you doing here?"

Surprise registered on Angie's face. "Eve? I...I forgot that you worked here. I'm looking for a girl named Molly Whitfield."

Eve's blood chilled. This was so not good. Before

she could sidetrack Angie, Molly responded with a big smile. "I'm Molly. How can I help you?"

Angie's eyes rested on Molly. For a long moment, Angie simply studied her. Molly's smile faltered. "Ma'am? Can I be of assistance?"

"I think you've given me enough assistance already."

Confusion replaced Molly's smile. "Have I met you?"

"You have not."

Eve intervened. "Angie. Why don't you come with me to my room? We can talk there."

"I can talk to her right here. I'm not staying long."

Molly looked from one to the other. "What do you want to talk about?"

"My husband."

"Your husband?"

"Don't act stupid."

A faint blush rose up Molly's neck, and Eve tried once more to head off the crisis. "Angie, I think I know where you're headed with this, but I'm pretty sure Molly doesn't."

Angie shifted Jessica to her hip and looked at Eve. "You knew? And you had the gall to come to my house for Thanksgiving?"

Eve shook her head. "No. I didn't know. Not then, anyway. Let's go to—"

"No." Angie turned back to Molly. "All I want is an explanation."

"For what, ma'am?"

Angie's mouth tightened. "For having an affair with my husband."

Molly blanched, and for a minute Eve thought the

girl might actually faint, but then she swallowed hard.

"Your husband?"

"God, you're good at playing innocent," Angie said. "You want me to spell it out? Okay, I will. My husband is a coach at Metro U. He's a friend of hers." Angie gestured to Eve. "His name is Chad Olson. Any of that ring a bell?"

Bewilderment spread over Molly's face. "I don't know a Chad Olson."

"You're lying."

Two red splotches of color formed on Molly's cheeks. "I don't lie."

Angie reached into her purse, and Eve tried to remember if Chad had ever said anything about owning a gun. She glanced down the deserted hall. Where was Security anyway? On coffee break? "Angie, please—"

"Here." Angie tossed a sheaf of papers on the desk in front of Molly. "Maybe those will refresh your memory."

Just a glimpse of the familiar format was all Eve needed to know what they were. She felt her own temper rise. Evidently when Trey had gotten hold of Brian's phone, he'd backtracked all of Eve's blogs as well and then managed to interface them, linking conversation with other contacts.

Molly's face turned ashen, and her hands trembled as she picked up the papers. "How…where did you get these?"

"They came in the mail today with an anonymous note."

"But…these are from my boyfriend. Chad *Jensen*."

Angie rolled her eyes. "Oh, for God's sake."

She dug in her purse again, and Eve reminded

herself Angie was holding Jessica. Surely, she wouldn't pull a weapon with her child on one hip. Where in bloody hell was Security? Eve widened her stance, wishing she'd taken self-defense at some point. Still, she could at least knock Angie off balance if she had to. To Eve's relief, Angie took out her wallet, flipping it open to reveal a picture of Chad.

"Is that him?"

Molly's pallor slipped to freshly fallen snow, her eyes dilating to near black. "How...why..." Her hands flew to cover her mouth. "It...it can't be."

"Well, it is." Angie snapped the wallet shut and snatched the papers back. "And you know what? You can keep him. I'm going to my mother's in Austin. When I'm finished with that bastard, he won't be sending you flowers anymore. He won't even have enough money left to buy coffee."

"There's got to be some mistake."

"No mistake, home wrecker."

"No! No, I'm not! I'm not a home wrecker! Wait!" Molly cried as Angie turned toward the door. "Please, wait..." But her plea fell on empty space as Angie didn't even look back as she walked out.

"I'm not a home wrecker!" Tears streamed down Molly's face as she stumbled to her feet, knocking over her chair. She turned and ran down the hall, nearly bumping into Joni ambling back from the teachers' lounge, a huge piece of cake in one hand. Joni stopped to stare at her and then turned to Eve.

"What's going on?"

But Eve just shook her head. She wasn't about to introduce new scandal. Use of Blog-Face had already done enough damage. At least things couldn't get any worse.

****

"Trying to drown your sorrows isn't going to make them go away," Eve said as she watched Chad chug his fifth beer Thursday afternoon at their favorite hangout.

"It will for a little while."

"You're going to have a massive hangover for workouts tomorrow."

"To hell with them."

"At least eat something." She pushed a bowl of peanuts and another of popcorn toward him. "How about some nachos?"

"I'm not hungry." Chad peered into his empty mug as though he were expecting it to magically refill. He motioned to the bartender. "Maybe just one more beer, though."

Eve caught the guy's eye and moved her head slightly.

"Hey, dude," the bartender said, "I'd like to serve you, but you're over the limit for the time you've been here."

"Damn it. I want a beer."

"Sorry. We've got a policy about not letting people get loaded."

"Bring us some nachos, please," Eve said.

"Sure thing."

"Damn it," Chad said again as the young man moved away. "Anything left in your martini glass?"

"Nope." Eve tilted it toward him. "Empty." She nudged the peanuts closer. "Eat. And let's talk."

"I don't want to."

"You need to, and you know it."

Eve knew she was being harsh, and for a minute she

193

thought Chad would get up and leave, but then he reached for a handful of peanuts.

"Angie left me." His brows knit together in consternation. "I didn't think she'd ever do that."

"She was hurt and angry. Give her some time."

"I don't think that's going to work."

"How do you know?"

"She's already contacted an attorney. I got a call this afternoon."

"That was quick."

"Even worse, it's Altman of Altman and Prescott."

Eve hid her surprise. The law firm had a reputation for being lethal in divorce cases. Even though Texas was a no-contest state, those attorneys were ruthless if adultery played a factor. Several well-known philanderers in the Metroplex over the past few years had even had their fortunes wiped out. Angie hadn't been kidding. "I am so sorry."

"Not as sorry as I am."

Eve decided not to comment on that, wishing she could order another martini. Instead she nibbled on a cheese-and-bean nacho and waited.

"Hell," Chad finally said. "What am I going to do?"

"Tough question. Tougher answer, I suspect." Eve shoved the plate in front of him. "Have you talked to Molly?"

"Yeah. Last night." He cringed. "She wants nothing to do with me."

"Ummm."

Chad frowned. "Just say it."

"I'm not sure it's my place to criticize."

"Maybe not, but what difference does that make? Go ahead."

"You shouldn't have gotten involved with Molly. You knew how naïve she was."

"Yeah, but that was what kept me interested."

Eve didn't try to hide her surprise this time. "You took advantage of her on purpose? That's pretty low."

"I didn't mean it that way. It's hard to explain. At first, I liked the idea that she was a virgin. I'd never had one. But then...then, I don't know. I became intrigued. She was so innocent. So *vulnerable*. Hell, she even compared me to a damn knight." Chad took another handful of peanuts. "And damn, if I didn't like it. For the first time in my life, I felt protective."

Eve couldn't have been more startled. "You actually *cared* about Molly?"

"I guess I did." Chad hesitated. "Actually, I think I was falling God-damn in love with her. Not that it's going to do me any good now. She doesn't ever want to hear from me again. She even deleted her Blog-Face account."

"I'm sorry," Eve said, "but at least you know you're capable of caring, maybe even loving." It was her turn to pause. "Maybe you should try and convince Angie of that. There's Jessica to consider."

Chad raised bleary eyes to Eve. "Do you think I have a chance?"

"You won't know until you try. Just be sure you mean it." She stood to leave. "Come on, I'll give you a ride home. We can pick up your car tomorrow."

Chad stood, wobbled a bit, and put a steadying hand on the counter. "Did anyone ever tell you that you're a good friend?"

"Yeah, well, you can return the favor one day."

"Too bad we aren't friends with benefits, though."

"Lack of benefits is *why* we're friends." Eve shook her head, wondering if there was any hope for Chad after all.

****

Finally, Friday. Two more hours before early release for the holidays. Molly had thought the day would never come, even though her world had fallen apart only two days before. She still felt numb.

"You doing all right?" Joni asked.

Molly nodded. What good would it do to say she felt like she'd been stabbed and the wound had not been stitched shut? Joni had managed to pry out what had happened and had offered sympathy—which made the seemingly never-ending fountain of tears flow again—along with a tirade about scum of the earth who used Blog-Face to lure and deceive their victims. Molly had never considered herself a victim before.

"I'll be fine when I get home. I'm heading out this afternoon." There was no point staying until Sunday now. Since she'd closed her blog account, Chad had left a couple of voicemails, but she didn't even want to listen to those, let alone answer them. She certainly didn't want him showing up at her apartment, either. The sooner she put distance between the two of them, the better.

"Yeah, it'll be good to be with your family."

"I'm looking forward to it." Which was only partially true. Goodness, she hoped she wasn't learning to become a liar. There wasn't any way she could tell her family what had happened, though. Her father hadn't approved of meeting someone on-line in the first place, and if he—or Mom—ever found out the man was married, they'd insist she move back to Calle Verde.

In spite of what had happened, Molly didn't want to

return to small town life. She'd been gullible and trusting. Next time—and there would be no more next time using any social media—she would be more careful.

"I think we'll survive," Miss O'Connor said as she put the end-of-semester paperwork that Mrs. Wilson required in the basket on the counter. Molly knew Eve meant the last two hours of school, but surprisingly enough, it had been Miss O'Connor—Eve—who had helped Molly survive those first few hours after discovering she'd been lied to and betrayed.

Miss O'Connor—Eve—had been lied to and betrayed as well, although it wasn't in the form of adultery. Even though Molly couldn't understand how Eve could condone an affair with a married man, she'd also begun to see that she should not judge without knowing all the facts. Eve had given Molly a glimpse into Chad's background as well, telling her it didn't excuse his actions, but that he truly wasn't the ogre Molly was building in her mind.

"No sense in risking our lives, though, until the students clear the parking lot," Arthur Conrad responded as he came up behind Eve with his own batch of papers.

"True. I sometimes think the kids can leave the parking lot faster than a first responder could get here." Eve turned to Molly. "Make sure you have a safe trip."

"I will. And…thanks for everything."

"No problem." Eve turned to the others and waved. "Have a good holiday."

"She seems to have recovered quickly," Joni said as they watched Eve go down the hall to her room.

"She's a survivor," Arthur said, "and a good person, in spite of what happened or what you might think."

"Oh." Joni's face turned red. "I didn't mean... Ah, I'd better get these papers to Mrs. Wilson before she comes looking." She got up so quickly she almost overturned her chair.

"I agree," Molly said after Joni had gone. "Miss O'Connor—Eve—helped me with...er, a problem."

Arthur studied her. "I heard."

Molly felt her face grow hot. "Oh, gosh. Does everyone know?"

"Probably not. I was waiting in the assistant principal's office." He gestured toward a door at the other end of the pigeonholes. "I heard the conversation."

"Oh," Molly said again, sure her face was on fire now. "I...I'm so sorry. I hope you don't think too badly of me."

"Not at all," Arthur replied. "It wasn't your fault. I'm sorry you were deceived. Some men are jerks. I hope you won't judge all of us that way."

"I...no, I won't. But..." Molly paused, not sure if she should go on. "I don't think I'll be so quick to commit to anything next time."

"Smart. Relationships take time to develop," Arthur replied and tilted his head, his brown eyes warm. "Perhaps when we get back from the holidays, I could buy you a cup of coffee?"

Molly stared at Arthur in surprise.

"It's just a cup of coffee. I thought... But if you don't want to—"

"No," Molly said quickly. "I mean, yes." Warmth spread through her body. Nothing tingly. Just very pleasant. "I think I would like that very much."

Arthur smiled. "To a new year, then."

Molly returned the smile. "To a new year."

****

Eve tossed her bag on her coffee table and collapsed unto the sofa. With early dismissal, it was only three o'clock, usually her most energetic time. Today, though, she felt like she'd stepped out of one of Rubens' more violent paintings—or perhaps more accurately, Falconet's *Punishment of Cupid*—and she hadn't emerged unscathed. Right after the final bell had rung, she'd been summoned to the principal's office again, this time to be told a report of the disastrous mess would be put on her permanent record.

Just what she needed to end a week that had included every layer of Dante's hell.

The only bright spot of the week had been Trey's absence from school, but even that had dimmed this morning when Brian sent her a blog saying a warrant had been issued for Trey's arrest due to the hacking. Eve still had to respond to that.

She had conflicting emotions. On the one hand, the kid had definitely done wrong, both in pilfering information from his father's blog and for breaking into the school's computer system. On the other hand, if Trey suspected his father was cheating—she hadn't been Brian's first mistress—then the kid was trying to correct a wrong, albeit in the *wrong* way.

Had it been *wrong* for her to get involved with Brian? Eve shook her head to clear it of all the "wrongs" circling in her mind. All she'd wanted was a good sex partner and maybe some intelligent conversation to go along with the bed play. If things had gone according to plan, no one would have been the wiser.

But things had gone awfully wrong—there was that word again!—and not just for her. Chad was in an even bigger, more serious mess, and that poor kid, Molly, had most of her illusions shattered. Betrayal and deceit were large, bitter pills to swallow.

But hadn't Eve been a participant in betrayal and deceit too?

She reached for her bag, pulled out her phone, and tapped Brian's message.

—Just got home. What horrible news.—

—Yeah. Brenda's a basket case.—

—Does she *know*?—

—Not about us. Warrant is for breaking into computer system.—

—Bit of sunshine then. You don't need to deal with both issues.—

—What I *need* is you. Can I come over?—

—Right now you need to deal with Trey's problem.—

Even as Eve typed it, she realized how true it was. Lord, she'd just told Chad yesterday that Jessica needed him—that his daughter was worth trying to make it right with Angie. Was this situation any different?

—I can deal with him later.—

—Deal with him now.—

—Why? The problem isn't going away.—

—Exactly.—

—Come on, babe. You know we'll both feel better after a roll.—

—Probably, but our problem isn't going away either.—

—Problem?—

—Us. Trey knows. We can't just continue.—

—Sure we can. We'll just be more careful.—

—You're missing the point.—

—Point?—

—Adultery. Betrayal. Deceit. Too many people get hurt.—

—What's gotten into you? We make great music together.—

—True, but there are other people in the chorus.—

—Metaphors aside, my wife isn't that interested in me.—

—Maybe not, but Trey is.—

—He's a kid.—

—A kid that needs you more than I do.—

—Don't tell me you'd break off what we have going.—

Eve hesitated. This was it, then. *Her* decision. Was she brave enough to make it?

—Eve? Let me come over, babe. I'll remind you how good it is.—

She didn't have to be reminded.

—Sorry. I really am, but you need to take care of your family.—

—Don't do this. You've just had a bad week.—

—So have your wife and son. Your duty lies with them.—

—I'll do my duty. I want you, babe.—

—You can't have both. I am truly sorry.—

—You're upset. I'll blog next week after you've had time to think.—

—Please don't. It's been good. Truly. *Slàinte.*—

Eve logged off before he could reply or she could change her mind. Would she be strong enough to resist Brian's blog next week? She could do what Molly had done. Slowly, Eve raised her finger and paused, staring at her phone as though it might answer the question for her. Then she tapped Delete.

Are you sure you want to delete this account?

Eve took a deep breath, then hit the Yes button.

She tossed the phone back in the bag. No more Brian. No more blog account.

Blog-Face—like her bedroom escapades—was all blarney anyway.

Epilogue

I laid the *Dallas Morning News* down, not feeling the usual elation I normally did when things turned out the way I predicted. Or, to be totally honest—a condition I rarely adhered to—the way I influenced events.

THE GRINCH WHO STOLE CHRISTMAS
AT DEER HILL HIGH

It was the lead story in the Local section. The school's computer system had been hacked by a student, and in the wake of the incident a whole plethora of other abuses had come to light. Not only was a teacher facing a disciplinary reprimand for having an affair with the hacker's father, but the father—Athletic Director at Metro U—was being arraigned on fraudulent expenses reported both by himself and a subordinate coach. The coach's wife had filed for divorce after finding out her husband was involved with a secretary at the same school.

Grinch indeed.

The Caldwell boy had been so easy to manipulate, filled with anger and resentment as he was. Certainly, it was convenient for me that he was such an expert in using a medium that humans thought was secure and safe.

Nothing is secure and safe. Nothing.

Yet mortals think they are infallible, blurting out on social media whatever comes to mind. Why would anyone think discussing plans best left for private discussion and describing personal desires or fantasies best left for bedrooms would remain private?

Nothing is secure and safe. Nothing.

When it comes to lust, though, mortals are fools.

Still, perhaps I was a bit too enthusiastic in bringing this simple fact to light.

Being tried in criminal court and being sued in civil court might be too much reparation for a teenager's retaliation to the action of his father.

Perhaps I will try to make amends, although, like honesty, it's a trait to which I rarely succumb.

I shall have to think on it.

Meanwhile, remember that your secrets, once shared, are not your own.

Loki

A word about the author…

Cynthia Breeding lives on the Gulf Coast of Texas with a very non-spoiled poodle-mix and enjoys walking and horseback-riding on the beach, as well as sailing.

www.cynthiabreeding.com